VAMPIRE MAKER

ALSO BY
MICHAEL SCHIEFELBEIN

Vampire Vow

Vampire Thrall

Blood Brothers

Vampire Transgression

Body and Blood

VAMPIRE MAKER

MICHAEL SCHIEFELBEIN

ST. MARTIN'S PRESS ☙ NEW YORK

This is a work of fiction. All of the characters, organizations, and events portrayed in this novel are either products of the author's imagination or are used fictitiously.

VAMPIRE MAKER. Copyright © 2009 by Michael Schiefelbein. All rights reserved. Printed in the United States of America. For information, address St. Martin's Press, 175 Fifth Avenue, New York, N.Y. 10010.

www.stmartins.com

Library of Congress Cataloging-in-Publication Data

Schiefelbein, Michael E.
  Vampire maker / Michael Schiefelbein. — 1st ed.
     p. cm.
  ISBN 978-0-312-36319-2
  1. Vampires—Fiction.   2. Gay men—Fiction.   I. Title.
  PS3619.C36V355 2010
  813'.6—dc22

                             2009033577

First Edition: January 2010

10 9 8 7 6 5 4 3 2 1

PART I

INFERNO

Per me si va nella città dolente

(Through me the way to the woeful city)

—DANTE ALIGHIERI *(Sign on the gate of Hell)*

1

Charles Boisvert chained his red Vespa to a balcony's iron support and stepped out onto Rampart Street, the northern boundary of the French Quarter.

The air was heavy with humidity. Wind shook the trees in Armstrong Park across the street. The lamps in the median were still not working after Hurricane Katrina and the neighborhood lay in darkness. But lightning continued to flash on the shuttered shotgun houses and nineteenth-century buildings with their wrought iron balconies. An occasional illumined window and hanging fern announced that a few occupants had returned to their homes after the evacuation.

Charles's big brown eyes gazed wistfully at the houses. Would New Orleans come back to life? That's what everyone asked. Would everyone return to the abandoned neighborhoods? Find jobs again? Rebuild their houses and their lives? Charles believed they would. Every day at Mass, he prayed they would. New Orleans was his hometown, and he would never lose hope that it would rise from the dead like Christ.

Charles wore a black clerical shirt with a Roman collar that hugged his thick neck. His ash-blond hair curled up at the back of the collar and over his ears. He was in his mid-twenties, and his good looks reflected his good nature. He had the kind of face that makes a good-looking man approachable—open, accepting, unpretentious, and even tempered—the face of a self-effacing athlete. His young body was athletic, too, his back and shoulders broad as a linebacker's, his furry forearms thick and strong, his hands big and square.

"Father Boisvert?"

The sonorous voice behind Charles took him by surprise. He'd heard no one approaching. He turned to find a tall, brown woman behind him. She was serene and graceful, draped in a printed orange tunic that fell to her ankles. Gold brocade adorned the tunic's scooped neckline, revealing her ample bosom. She wore her hair in dreadlocks, gathered at the nape of her neck into an abundant cataract that fell down her back.

"Yes." Charles nodded. "Can I help you?"

"I'm Dr. Beauchamp."

Charles recognized the name. When the woman extended her hand, Charles shook it.

"I was just taking a stroll before the rain started." A hint of a Caribbean accent was in her voice. "I saw your Roman collar. I thought it must be you."

Charles had noted the accent in his extended phone conversation with Dr. Beauchamp the week before, but he had not pictured such a beautiful woman, so magnificently Caribbean. Instead, her clinical observations on the phone and the formality of their discussion had summoned the image of a woman in a white lab coat, her hair cropped close—peering at him through horn-rimmed glasses.

An advertisement in a conservative religious magazine had led him to Dr. Beauchamp. It invited Roman Catholics to enter treatment to prevent relapses into moral disorders decried by the Church. "Science and Faith can work together," the ad had announced. "Discover your strength to be a faithful Catholic."

The ad had seemed to call him by name. Uncannily, it seemed intended for his unique situation. And when he had spoken to Dr. Beauchamp on the phone, she seemed to recognize perfectly his needs—though he provided few details. She told him to hold the information for his first session. She promised him that, whatever the facts, she could help. And he did not doubt her. The connection between them had seemed profound, even mysterious. He felt that God had sent her to him.

Charles and Dr. Beauchamp had walked less than a block when they arrived at her office, a renovated shotgun house with bright blue shutters. Beauchamp opened the door and led him into a dimly lit room with a high ceiling.

On the wall above a computer station hung an African rendition of the Virgin Mary that bore a remarkable resemblance to Dr. Beauchamp. She was wrapped in a bright orange printed garment, and she swaddled her shiny baby in a cloth of royal blue. Her broad nose was pierced by three rings. She stared serenely ahead like a tribal queen.

On one side of the room, floor-to-ceiling shelves displayed more African art—elongated statues carved from dark wood, stylized masks, brightly painted crockery, and baskets. On the opposing wall hung a blanket with a green and white African print. Behind Charles, dark leather chairs were arranged around a glass table, draped with a woven African runner.

"Please have a seat here at the computer, and let me explain this device."

Charles sat down and listened to Dr. Beauchamp's instructions, blushing as she indicated how he was to attach the device to his penis and how the square plethysmograph would record his responses to the photos as they flashed on the screen. He was relieved when she finally left him alone, disappearing to an office at the rear of the building.

Charles positioned himself as directed, unzipped his pants, attached the device to his penis, and viewed the first image. It was a close-up of a wrestling match. The shaggy-haired blond in the photo squeezed the shaved head of his opponent in the crook of his powerful arm.

Charles felt nothing on viewing the image. He was relieved. He relaxed, leaning back in the chair, his broad back butterflied against the chair rest, his massive thighs spread on the seat, and his strong, furry arms rested confidently on the arms of the chair. His big hand worked the computer mouse, his finger clicking through more images: two shirtless movie idols, an Asian man in a thong, and a beautiful boy stretched out on the beach. None of the images troubled Charles, but he occasionally glanced at his penis and the machine registering his reactions.

When he finished viewing the photos, he removed the device, zipped his pants, got up, and opened the door near the computer table.

"Finished, Dr. Beauchamp," he called down the dark hallway.

A door at the back of the building opened, and the tall silhouette of Dr. Beauchamp appeared. She approached him, and he stood aside to let her in.

"Please, Father Boisvert," she said, stretching her long, smooth arm toward the seating area behind him. "Make yourself comfortable."

Charles sat in an armchair. Dr. Beauchamp tore the report from the plethysmograph and took a seat across from him on the sofa, crossing her legs and sitting back to study the results.

"This looks good," she said, nodding. "Did you have to concentrate very hard to keep from responding?"

Charles grinned and shook his head. "I think I was a little self-conscious."

"Of course. That's to be expected your first time. As you relax, your body will respond naturally."

"Or unnaturally," Charles admitted with good-natured resignation.

Dr. Beauchamp nodded approvingly. "I'm happy you respect Church teaching. Many people have accepted the relativism of secular society. Even some priests have. It's good to see a newly ordained priest with your values. I must tell you, that as a faithful Catholic, I would not have accepted you as a client had you told me you were trying to make peace with your orientation. I'm even willing to use methods not approved by my professional associations." She held up the plethysmograph results. "I'm happy you agreed with my program. In our phone interview, you promised to tell me your story. Why don't you go ahead now?"

Charles nodded. "Well, like I said on the phone. I was just ordained in June for the Archdiocese of New Orleans, and I've been assigned to St. Louis Cathedral."

"What a wonderful first placement. Quite a privilege."

Charles nodded in agreement. "What are the odds that a mediocre seminarian ends up in the cathedral?"

"I'm sure academic credentials don't much matter. It's piety that counts."

Charles shrugged. "Maybe. But I wasn't always pious."

"Tell me about your upbringing."

"Well, my family was Catholic. But who isn't in New Orleans? We had religious pictures and rosaries around the house. Went to Mass most Sundays. At least, my mother did. My dad was usually catching up on his sleep. He's a plumber. My little brother and I went to Catholic schools. Then I went to New Orleans U. I was pretty wild. Drank a lot on the weekends. Made the rounds at the gay bars on Bourbon Street. Having lots of unsafe sex. I was lucky for the first three years. Then I got a call from the Health Department. A guy I'd been with had given them my name to contact, when he got his results."

"So, you're HIV positive?" Dr. Beauchamp said.

"That's what I thought. Jesus, I *knew* I was. I'd had sex with the guy enough, in all the right ways. I was scared to death. For the first time in years I started going to Mass—every day. Started saying the rosary. I wanted to change my life. I promised God that I'd stop disobeying the Church if I could just test negative. I mean the Church's teaching about homosexuality. I'd go through one of those ex-gay programs. I'd quit being gay. I prayed like a saint for almost a month before I finally got the nerve to get tested. And when I did, I was negative for HIV."

"You must have been incredibly relieved."

"Hell yes! Ran to church, fell down on my knees and thanked God." Charles paused. "But you know what they say about the road to hell. It's paved with good intentions."

"You strayed?"

"For a month I stayed on the wagon. Then I got horny. Lonely. It was final exam time, very stressful. It was hot and muggy out. I left my folks' house in the Marigny and took a walk through the Quarter. Café Du Monde was packed with tourists. The tarot card readers and artists had lots of customers on Jackson Square. I just wanted to be with people having a good time. I found myself strolling toward Bourbon Street. I figured I'd just have a drink at a bar. What could it hurt? I'd behave. I'd look, but not touch, if you know what I mean." Charles sighed. "Of course it didn't work. The spirit is willing, but the flesh is weak. I went home with a lumberjack type. It was probably the best sex I ever had.

"On the way home, I puked. I'd had a lot to drink. I felt like I'd betrayed God. Broke my promise. As I walked down St. Peter's alongside the cathedral, I felt like someone was walking behind me, right on my heels. I turned around. But there was no one in sight. Then it dawned on me how quiet everything seemed. I didn't hear music or voices from Jackson Square. I didn't hear any cars. And when I came to the backside of the cathedral on Royal Street, it was deserted. Usually there's an artist there, with pictures hung up on the fence around the church grounds. But the street was completely empty. Then someone called out my name. 'Charles, my son, you are mine. Be healed.' I can still hear that voice, clear as a bell. I looked up through the bars of the fence at the statue of Jesus inside the courtyard. Jesus's hands were stretched out as always, but they moved toward me, like I was a baby that he wanted to pick up. My chest got warm. As though I'd had a shot of whiskey. I thought I couldn't be seeing what I was seeing. The statue glowed and moved toward me, and by the time it got to the fence, I could see it wasn't a statue. It was a man. He was as white as the statue had been. But he was real. And I fell to my knees on the sidewalk. And I said, 'My Lord and my God.'"

Charles paused, as though waiting for a sign of Dr. Beauchamp's incredulity. But it didn't come.

"An apparition," she said, studying him. "You were favored."

Charles nodded solemnly. "And I knew I was cured of being gay! I could feel it in my gut. This incredible current of strength rushed through me like a river. My head was clear even after all the drinking. I didn't feel the least bit sick. I wanted to prove to myself that I was cured. I ran back to the bar where I'd met the guy I'd slept with. I stood by the wall, looking over every attractive guy to see what would happen. There was a hunk in a tank top, and a guy with a swimmer's body—lean and sinewy—and a beautiful kid with a long ponytail. Didn't feel a thing! I even tried to get excited, staring at their crotches and butts—but nothing happened.

"Over the next few days I was on a high. As I sat in class, I felt like Superman. Invincible! None of the guys in the class could turn my head. My mind stayed on Christ, his words to me. I felt his love. I felt him calling me. And the feeling didn't die. It just got stronger day after day and week after week. And so I decided to give my life to God. I'd become a priest. I talked to the vocations director of the archdiocese. He was great. Happy to have me. He gave me all of the application stuff. I worried that somehow the director would look at me and know the things I'd done. I promised God I'd stay on the right path, if I got accepted. I wouldn't take my cure for granted. I promised I'd go to a counselor for direction."

"Very wise, Charles—not to presume on the powers of God. We must cooperate with grace. Your decision to monitor yourself was a good one."

Charles didn't put up an argument.

"Please go on."

Charles shrugged. "Not much left to tell. I was accepted by the archdiocese. They sent me to seminary in Rome. That was four years ago. Got ordained at the cathedral in June. Katrina hit in August. And we're all still trying to pick up the pieces."

"Your family has returned? Since they live in the Marigny—where there was little flooding."

"We all spent the last couple of months with relatives in Houston. But everyone's back. Dad's got plenty of plumbing work. Mom cleans hotels in the Quarter. The cathedral is up and running."

"And have your temptations recurred?" Beauchamp said.

"No, not at all. Every now and then, I stare at a good-looking guy, just to check myself. I hope I'm not putting the Lord to the test. I don't feel a twinge of attraction. Just detachment. Oh, he's a good-looking guy, I think—just the way a straight guy might notice that a guy is handsome. Christ gave me the power. So, you believe me, Doc? You don't think I'm nuts?"

Beauchamp did not flinch. "God acts in mysterious ways. I've known others with visions. With cures, if you will. My faith tells me these things are possible. For those who believe, all things are possible."

A sudden flash of lightning brightened the window. A bolt of thunder rattled the statues on the shelves.

"I guess I should take off before it pours," Charles said, rising.

Dr. Beauchamp remained seated. She raised her hand. "One last thing. While you were in Rome . . . you underwent therapy?"

Charles nodded. "But nothing like this. Just counseling. The therapist was a priest. I told him about my cure and how I wanted to keep myself monitored. He was pretty doubtful at first. Thought I was just stifling my attractions. His approach was that you should face attractions so they never overtake you. Every now and then, he'd ask me if I'd had sexual fantasies or dreams. I always said no. I think he started to believe me. He could see how happy I was. We talked about normal problems—stress, conflicts with pastors at the churches where I interned."

"That's wonderful," Dr. Beauchamp said. "I hope my form of monitoring you doesn't seem outrageous. I believe in it. And I think that now that you are ordained, away from the supportive environment of a seminary, you must be very proactive about the possible dangers of temptation."

Charles grinned, rising to his feet. "I'm in your hands, Doc. I think that's the way Christ wants it."

Smiling, Dr. Beauchamp stood and showed him to the door, where he smiled and thanked her for the session.

Hurrying up the street to his bike, Charles unlocked it, climbed on, and tore off to beat the rain. It was Halloween, the eve of All Saints' Day, and he was scheduled to hear confessions at seven and say the Holy Day vigil Mass at seven thirty. He'd gone only three blocks when the sky let loose. In the downpour he almost struck a man crossing the street. When he hit the brakes, the man stopped and turned his head. The light from the bike shone on a face that seemed preternaturally white. The weird lividness startled Charles. The man resumed walking, and Charles figured the strange pallor was due to his strong headlight.

His clothes were drenched by the time he reached the triple peaks of the cathedral's façade. He locked up the bike and entered the vestibule of the church. The sexton had opened the doors and turned on the lights. When Charles passed through the double doors into the nave, he dipped his hand into the bowl of holy water held by a stone cherub and blessed himself.

A dozen people, most of them kneeling, were scattered among the rows and rows of dark pews, and a girl with tattooed arms was lighting a votive candle in the glowing racks in the front of the nave. The church was built in the late eighteenth century when New Orleans was under French rule. On both sides of the nave, columns supported galleries, and high above the nave rose a vault adorned with painted vignettes. In the center vignette, Christ handed keys to the kingdom to St. Peter. In the apse a marble reredos rose above the golden tabernacle. The words *Ecce Panis Angelorum* were etched in the pediment of the reredos. And above it was a painting of King Louis IX and his grand court with attending priests.

Charles traveled down the marble center aisle, genuflected before the tabernacle, and entered the sacristy on the side of the elevated sanctuary. There he removed his clerical shirt and donned a cassock he found in the closet. He removed a stole from one of the long, thin doors in the oak wardrobe, kissed it, and placed it around his neck before going to the confessional at the back of the church. Several people had already lined up in expectation. Charles avoided looking them in the face as he entered his side of the confessional. A priest had to respect the anonymity of the confessional the best he could.

The first two penitents, an elderly woman and a young father, rattled off a grocery list of sins. Charles assigned the penances, absolved the individuals, and quickly sent them on their way. Then came the third person to enter the chamber on the other side. Whoever it was hesitated to speak.

"You okay?" Charles said.

"Yes," a man responded, then hesitated again. "No. I'm not. I'm in hell, Father."

"In hell?" Charles frowned and leaned forward toward the dark panel where not even the outline of the man kneeling on the other side was visible.

"Yes. If I don't escape, I'll be damned. But I can't escape. And I don't want to escape."

"Look," Charles said, "I don't have a clue what you're talking about. I'm a pretty simple guy. You have to give it to me straight."

"You can't help me."

"Well, I think you're wrong about that," Charles said emphatically, determined to reach out to this troubled soul. "You must think so, too, or you wouldn't be here. What do you want to escape from? Your marriage? Addiction? Listen, I've heard it all. You don't have to worry about shocking me."

"From him!"

By the tone of the young man's voice, Charles sensed that he was moving into territory too close to home. He shifted uncomfortably, moving back in his seat to distance himself. "Who is this guy?" he said. "Your lover?"

The man didn't seem to hear the question. "He tells me when I can come and when I can go. He tells me what I can feel. I'm at his beck and call. And I want to be. I can't help it."

"I'm not getting this," Charles said, confused. "Does he beat you or something? If he does, you can find protection. The cops are back in New Orleans. You can go to them."

The man behind the panel said nothing.

"What's your name?"

"Kyle," the man whispered.

"Kyle, you've done the right thing to come here. You don't have to feel guilty. If this guy is abusing you, it's not your fault—if that's what you think. You're not morally culpable."

Kyle emitted something between a laugh and a sob. "It's no use. I can't begin to explain. You wouldn't believe me if I could."

"Give me a chance," Charles pleaded, worried that the man sounded desperate.

The man paused. "Have you ever swallowed blood, Father? Have you ever craved it so much, you might even kill for it?"

The words left Charles stunned. He wondered if the man was dangerous.

"You see what I mean? How can you understand anything about me?"

Charles collected himself and proceeded. "But you're here. You want to tell me. So, what's this about blood? You talking about revenge?"

"There's no one I *want* to hurt. I just do. I'm trapped here."

"Katrina has devastated lots of lives," Charles ventured. "You've got every reason to want to strike out at somebody. We all do."

"But I *don't* want to strike out. I want to be taken. I want to be lost."

The declaration sent a chill up Charles's spine. Who could *want* to be lost? He had to reason with this man, and that required time. But he'd have to get ready for Mass soon. Charles held his wristwatch close to the dim light in his side of the confessional. It was 7:25. "It's time for Mass to begin," he said, reluctant to dismiss the man. "But I'll come back afterwards. We can talk more. Are you sorry for your sins?"

"Yes," the man said, softly.

Charles absolved him and waited for him to leave the confessional before switching off the light and climbing out himself. As he hurried to the sacristy, he scanned the people in the pews. There were fifty or so now. One of these people was the strange penitent, but out of respect for the anonymity of the confessional, as worried as he was about the man, he didn't let himself search their faces. He quickly vested and proceeded to the sanctuary, where he genuflected, kissed the altar, and walked to the presider's chair.

Facing the congregation, he noticed the face almost immediately. The livid face that had glowed in the headlight of his Vespa. The man sitting in one of the front pews was young and boyish with shaggy white-blond hair, a square jaw, and full, pale lips.

Now, in the soft lights of the chandeliers, his pallor didn't seem as extreme as it had on the dark street, in the glare of the headlight. The man was clearly troubled. He clasped the pew in front of him as though to steady himself, lowering his eyes, as though to avoid Charles's gaze. Was this Kyle, the distressed penitent?

Throughout the first part of the Mass, Charles's gaze wandered to the man, who sat and listened and stood like everyone else during the ritual. But something strange happened at the moment of the consecration. As Charles lifted the white host above the altar, a fiercely handsome, dark-haired man walked through the central doors at the back of the nave. He was dressed in black—a turtleneck, leather jacket, jeans, and boots. He stared at Charles for a moment, arrogantly it seemed, but the distance was too great to be sure. Then his eyes roamed over the congregation until they fell on the section of the church where the troubled man was kneeling. And in the midst of the most solemn part of the Mass, he marched brazenly up the center aisle, and, without genuflecting, moved into Kyle's pew—surely it was Kyle—and sat down, stretching his arms across the back of the pew, as though to take everything in.

His face was even more livid than Kyle's.

Kneeling, Kyle shifted uncomfortably at the presence behind him, but he remained on his knees, his gaze focused on the altar where Charles now prepared to serve communion.

Accompanied by a young, dark-haired acolyte, Charles carried the golden ciborium to the steps of the sanctuary, where a line began to form. Some people extended their hands to receive the consecrated wafer. The more traditional communicants opened their mouths and extended their tongues to be fed. Charles waited for Kyle, but when the line of people dwindled, it was clear that Kyle was not planning to advance. However, the severe-looking man who sat next to Kyle suddenly stood and moved out of the pew to the side of the transept, where a large crucifix hung. He stared at the plaster corpus for a moment before turning and sauntering to the communion line. He was the final communicant. His defiant eyes remained on Charles as he received the host on his tongue. His eyes were bright and dark as polished stone, impossibly black, it seemed, against the alabaster skin, with its heavy bluish beard. He fixed his eyes on Charles. Unnerved, Charles almost dropped the ciborium.

Then the man turned away, spitting the host on the marble tile.

The action stunned Charles. He'd never seen anything so blasphemous in his life. Finally recovering himself, Charles stooped, collected the wafer from the floor, and swallowed it himself, the only thing to do with a desecrated host—apart from burying it. When he turned, the little acolyte looked shaken. His freckled face was pale, and his chocolate eyes were wide.

"It's all right," Charles whispered. He guided him back to the altar to clean the sacred vessels and conclude the Mass.

After the benediction, he exited down the aisle with the acolyte to the vestibule, where he greeted departing worshippers as they passed into the storm still raging over the dark streets of the Quarter. No one remarked on the awful scene at the communion rail. Probably no one had seen it. Most of the congregation had been kneeling in their pews, their eyes closed as they offered prayers of thanksgiving. When Charles had shaken the hand of the last departing person, he moved back into the church to seek the two strangers. At first there was no sign of Kyle and his companion. But as the edge of the transept came into view, he saw them both standing under the crucifix. The fierce man in black clenched Kyle by the back of his neck. He seemed to be directing Kyle's gaze toward the bowed head of the dying Christ. Everything in the man's posture, everything in the way he spoke into Kyle's face, announced his profound ability to control someone he deemed a protégé, and one who had failed to live up to the mark.

"It's from France," Charles said, indicating the crucifix. "The late eighteenth century."

"Fascinating," the man in black said, without deigning to glance at Charles.

"Let's go, Victor," Kyle pleaded.

"We're not through," the fierce man responded. "I want you to get your fill." He tightened his grip on Kyle's neck.

Charles stopped himself from rushing at this Victor and prying his hand away. An attack could have bad results for Kyle. Instead, he tried distraction. "Why did you do it?"

The technique worked. Victor released Kyle and turned to Charles, suddenly eyeing him with interest. "It," Victor said, spitting out the word as he'd spit out the sacred host, "disagreed with me."

"If you don't respect the Eucharist, you should stay away from churches." Unflinching, Charles folded his arms over his chasuble.

Victor laughed disdainfully, baring his teeth. For a split second, his flashing canines seemed elongated, and the sight unnerved Charles. He took a step back. Victor laughed again.

"You're welcome to stay with me," Charles said to Kyle, who'd turned from the crucifix. He hesitated to say more, for fear that Victor would punish Kyle for betraying his master. Charles might not have ventured saying even this much if he hadn't sensed the abuse that awaited Kyle in Victor's hands.

Now apprised of the transgression, Victor studied his protégé.

"Well, there's an interesting offer, Kyle. Do you want to go with this priest? What's your name, Father?"

"Charles Boisvert."

"And you've returned to your flock in New Orleans. You know, they say the water is still contaminated. They say there are still dead to recover. Are you sure you want to be in such a devastated city?"

"It's my home."

"Your family lives here?" Victor's eyes, black as onyx, were full of menace.

Charles did not favor him with a reply. He turned to Kyle. "Do you want to stay with me?"

His glance full of sad resignation, Kyle shook his head.

"You have your answer, Father." Victor placed his pale hand on Kyle's shoulder. "He's a grown man. He knows his own mind. But he might be back. He can't keep himself away from churches. It's an obsession of his."

"Maybe it's God's voice." Reassuringly, Charles directed the words to Kyle.

Kyle looked at him. His gray eyes were eerily feral, the eyes of a frightened wolf.

As Victor led his charge away, he touched Charles's cheek. His hand stung like ice. The church was not particularly cold, and even if it were, it could hardly explain Victor's chilled flesh. Or was Charles mistaken? After all, Victor's hand had barely brushed his face. Maybe Victor's cold heart had distorted every perception about Victor, even his sense of Victor's touch. If so, surely Victor's heart was the coldest Charles had ever encountered.

2

The shadows of dusk had descended on Lafayette Cemetery, but the names inscribed on the mausoleums were still easily discernible. This was true even of the worn name of Captain C. H. Kempt, who died "At Sea" in 1857, according to the epitaph. And it was true of the name of Maude Elaine Heuer, who died on December 12, 1842, evidently giving birth to Baby Evelyn, whose name appeared below hers, with the same date listed for her birth and death. Cities of the dead, they call the New Orleans cemeteries, and with good reason. The mausoleums rise like miniature mansions, some twelve or fifteen feet high, some with Greek columns and pediments, some enclosed by wrought-iron fences, some covered with English ivy. They stand shoulder to shoulder along paved lanes, under magnolias, still shiny and green in the November air. If the moldy inhabitants could slip from their shelves—stacked five or six or even twelve high—and heave open the tablets forming their doors, they might stroll through Lafayette's streets, within the privacy of the wall surrounding their one-square block in the Garden District, where their old manses, many of them antebellum, still stand.

In the breezy twilight, where magnolia leaves scraped along Lafayette's lanes, a sense of ghostly stirring rose, as though the spirits of the residents did amble arm in arm through their November city. But the disturbing presence did not belong to them. At the edge of the city of corpses, in an ivy-entangled tomb that rose fifteen feet to a fine Greek pediment engraved with the family name Boudreaux, the central iron door swung open and the handsome Victor stepped out. His death shroud was contemporary attire, a violet silk shirt, black jeans, and square-toed boots, hardly enough to keep a living man warm in a winter tomb—even in balmy New Orleans—once the sun has disappeared. But Victor was unconcerned about staying warm. Moreover, the sun was not far gone. Victor felt its lingering rays, though their source was no longer visible. He boldly lifted his face to absorb them, his eyes closed. He had never arisen when so much radiation suffused the air.

Securing the iron door of the tomb, he walked down the lane leading to the cemetery's gate and peered through it at Washington Street. The sidewalk revealed no signs of a pedestrian walking a dog or strolling to the market. The great houses opposite the cemetery were quiet. Many were still empty after the hurricane. Although the high ground of the Garden District spared them from flooding, city services had only just started returning full force, and residents had only begun trickling back from their refuges in the west or north. With hardly an effort, Victor sprang up eight feet onto the wall, surveying the street once more before dropping to the sidewalk. His nostrils distended. He smelled blood. His lips parted, and the long canines extended into fangs almost two inches long.

Less than a block away, in front of a Georgian mansion on Prytania, a woman chatted on her cell phone while her leashed German shepherd pawed the ground. At Victor's advance the black dog growled. With a fleeting glance at Victor, the middle-aged woman, in a rose mohair sweater and gray slacks, tugged the leash to quiet her animal. But the dog bared his teeth at Victor. Then, with a mere thought, hardly voluntary, let alone intense, Victor caused the dog to choke. The beast hacked as though a bone stuck in his throat. The woman slipped her phone into her pocket, and squatted, futilely cajoling her pet to cough up the obstruction.

"What's he choking on?" Victor said, squatting beside her.

"I don't know. I didn't see him swallow anything."

Victor directed another thought to the animal's mind. The beast stopped choking, stumbled, and fell, whining pitifully before going into convulsions that stopped abruptly.

"My God!" The woman touched the dog as though trying to wake him. "Shep!" For the first time, she looked into Victor's face and fell back fearfully when she saw his mouth.

He pounced on her throat and pierced her soft flesh. With the first drop of her blood on his tongue, she lost consciousness. He drank only as much as he required and no more. In his own neighborhood, he would leave no corpses. There was no need to do so, since the nourishment he required from each victim was not enough to kill and drinking from a victim did not render the victim a thrall. It did nothing but leave puncture marks, eventually discovered by the victim upon recovery of consciousness, which occurred with only the vague memory of an unpleasant sensation or dream, and with the alarmed sense of having suffered a seizure of some kind. New, impulsive, inexperienced vampires might drink too much in the pleasure of the moment, though even they stopped drinking when the victim's heart reached the dangerous slow beat that signaled death. Blood from a corpse was fatal to a vampire.

Victor stepped over the woman and smiled at the animal,

proud of his growing strength. His two-thousand-year-old mind had always been capable of controlling beasts, even killing them, but never with so little concentration.

He resumed walking, passing the dark Bradish Johnson House on Prytania. The massive structure, with its columns and mansard roof, sat securely behind an iron fence. He had attempted to buy the mansion when he and Kyle came to New Orleans four years ago, but it had been converted into a school for girls, and the board would not consider his generous offer. It had been just as well. He would have needed to build a wall around the place. The house was too exposed. The portico, the upper gallery, the long windows were completely visible, the large magnolias on the property confined to the perimeter. He needed a more hidden dwelling, one safe from the eyes of tourists who roamed the Garden District with their cameras, often led by guides with ghost stories to tell and vampire sightings to report—thanks to the author who had made her career on ridiculous fantasies about the undead. So, having his bid rejected was for the best. Still, he punished the representative of the school by feeding on him, a compulsive act of revenge that he indulged himself in. Why shouldn't he?

His strolled to his own abode on First Street, just a few blocks away. It was a Greek Revival mansion with four columns supporting a straight pediment. Behind the columns was a deep portico reached by marble stairs and a gallery above for the second floor. The long, shuttered windows were darkened by drapes. One could see the mansion only through iron gates at the entrance. A tall, ivy-covered wall enclosed the property, with thick bamboo and towering magnolias all around the house. He punched in the door code on the pad near the gate and the iron pales slowly parted and opened inward. He climbed the stairs and unlocked the front door.

Inside the dark front room, which stretched across the width of the house, he turned on a table lamp, and the faint light illumined the heavy furniture, upholstered in rich colors of damask and arranged in sitting areas. On the walls hung dark oil portraits that he had purchased from a plantation auction when he moved to New Orleans. Most of the portraits were grim family members from the plantation in nineteenth-century attire—cravats and stovepipe hats, lace caps and crinolines. Over the tall mantle hung a portrait of a raven-headed woman in a red gown, standing in profile with a parrot on her finger. Through an archway, the dining room table and buffet were visible under a shadowy chandelier. The table seated twenty people, and on rare occasions Victor assembled that number of guests from a list of those who used to frequent his club in Georgetown, a converted Gothic church that served the needs of those inclined to violent and daring sexual practices. He found the visitors entertaining. He enjoyed watching their attempts to seduce one another, and he enjoyed feeding on them in the big rooms upstairs and the guesthouse behind the mansion.

All was quiet. But he knew Kyle waited for him as commanded, and he climbed the central staircase to his bedroom. He found Kyle in the custom-made bed that he'd brought with him from Georgetown. The four posts were modeled on the columns of Bernini's baldacchino in St. Peter's Basilica. They twisted to the lofty ceiling like four coiled snakes. The furniture in the large room included heavy, upholstered chairs in scarlet and cream, tables, and a tall chest of drawers made of gleaming mahogany.

Victor removed his clothes and joined Kyle under the magenta sheets. He did his protégé no violence, indulging instead a sudden tenderness for the thrall he had created in Georgetown four years ago. The creation had been an act of appropriation, to hold in check a lover, now best forgotten. Kyle was then a young priest who had become infatuated with that erstwhile lover, and he had never succeeding in abandoning his piety, despite its futility. It would never secure him a place in heaven. Heaven was not for him any longer. As a thrall, he moved between the world of the living and the undead, completely at Victor's command, executing for his master tasks under the light of the sun, protecting him when necessary. Thralls were always dispensable, and Victor had dispensed with a number of them over the centuries—until he had discovered one that he longed to turn into his equal, in violation of certain cosmic laws against the association of vampires. The violation had devastating consequences, ultimately, his mandated separation from the vampire he had created. But Victor was beginning to understand other, beneficial consequences of his violation. A new level of power coursed through him, and in this moment it called forth if not his humane instincts—for had a onetime officer of the Roman Empire ever possessed soft sentiments?—then at least his whim to patronize and indulge. And so, he tenderly caressed Kyle, and took him in a way that the most protective, worshipful lover might have taken a girl whose maidenhead was intact.

As they lay side by side afterward, their chests still heaving, Victor took Kyle's hand and kissed it.

"Today, it was even earlier," he said. "When I opened the gate, I felt the rays. The sun wasn't completely down. There was a halo of light on the trees in Lafayette."

Kyle seemed to resist some unspoken implication of Victor's words. He turned his head on the pillow to face his master with earnest eyes. "I'm getting better. Last week was the first time I went to Mass in months. Since before the hurricane."

"That's only because there have been no Masses. Didn't I find you hovering around the cathedral twice? Haven't I come upon you kneeling on this floor with a rosary in your hand? It's been four years since your transformation. If you haven't lost your religious scruples by now, you never will."

"I'm a priest."

"*Was* a priest," Victor corrected. He could read the objection in Kyle's mind, the objection Kyle dared not voice because to do so would only make Victor's case. One is ordained forever. There's no retraction of the mystical change that occurs in a man's soul once the bishop has laid hands on him. *You are a priest forever, according to the order of Melchizedek.* "Now, about my proposition," Victor continued. "Have you been considering it?"

"It's why I went to Mass."

"To ask God for guidance?" Victor mocked.

"I don't know. It's what I've always done. You're right. I know you're right. You've turned me into what I am. I can't go back. But I can't go forward."

"Precisely. That's my point. There's only one way."

"But how can you be sure?" Kyle said fearfully. "How can you be sure that the Dark Kingdom won't demand that we separate? The way they made you separate from Paul?"

Victor tried to dismiss the feeling of tenderness that Paul's name still evoked. He was normally a master at maintaining the coldness of a killer. But passion was different from sentimentality. Passion for Paul he had known. The tenderness he felt now was a remnant of that passion.

But despite the distracting sensation, Victor managed an answer to Kyle's objection. "Then, I was under their power. Either I separated from Paul or they would destroy him. But then my own strength was not what it is now. I've told you. I lifted my head to the sun. With a simple thought, I took the life of an animal. The truth is this, Kyle. A vampire maker acquires new power. That's what I've learned. The Dark Kingdom knows it."

The Dark Kingdom was the cosmic realm that governed vampires—insofar as such rebellious beings can be governed. The Dark Kingdom was also the heaven of eternal bliss for vampires once they had served their term of two hundred years on the earth as nocturnal predators—and once each had replaced himself by creating another vampire. Not only *could* a vampire then ascend to the Dark Kingdom, but he *must* ascend there for the sake of cosmic balance of good and evil, victims and predators. At least, this was the reason that Victor had learned from agents of the Dark Kingdom. But now that he had rebelled, remaining on the earth after creating a vampire, he knew the true reason for the rule for ascending. Vampire makers grew in power, and in doing so, challenged the control the Dark Kingdom had over them.

"That's the real reason that we are required to ascend there, once we've created a new being like us," Victor continued. "All of this abstract rubbish about rules against the association of vampires for danger of concentrating our kind of power is true, but not for the reasons they give. They don't care about the universe's laws of balancing evil and good. They care about control. A vampire maker slips out of their control. And in that case, I can make another vampire and amass even more power."

"That's all you want, isn't it?" Kyle seemed disappointed. Despite himself, he clearly wanted more from Victor.

And deigning to reassure him that he had more to give, Victor caressed Kyle's cheek. "I want a lover with the strength to resist these urgings of yours. I want your whole heart. Not part of it. If you're my equal . . ."

"I'll never be," Kyle interrupted, eyeing him bitterly. "You don't want that."

"I'm not the frightened one, am I?" Victor reasoned.

Kyle remained silent for a moment. "What if you're wrong?"

"Why speculate?"

"Because if you're wrong, I'm left all alone. For two hundred years. That's the law. You told me so yourself. After two hundred years I can join you in the Dark Kingdom. If you choose to go there. And you didn't four years ago. So if you leave me alone, a being like you, I'll never see the day again. And I may never see you again." Kyle stared at Victor accusingly.

"Ah, but that's not what's really holding you back." Victor chucked Kyle under the cheek, playfully but with a clenched jaw. He felt like striking him.

Kyle turned his face away.

"You're afraid of damnation. And the wheel turns back to its starting point. This is always the issue with you. No matter how many times I remind you. There is no escaping the realm you inhabit. Your God can't draw you back into the other sphere. You're a new being. You should be happy you can live in the daylight. And that you don't have to feed as I feed, since it offends your moral sensibilities. Despite your cravings."

Victor intended the final remark as a dig. For just after transforming Kyle into his present state, Victor had forced him to watch his master feed just so he would know the craving he must not satisfy. Kyle had hungrily pounced on the victim's throat only to vomit the blood he had swallowed. "You desire it, but you can't have it," Victor had told Kyle, who was still on his hands and knees by the victim's bed. "The blood you need comes only from me." He had proceeded to offer Kyle his wrist, which he slit with his sharp nail. And Kyle had sucked like a foal.

"Why cling to a fantasy?" Victor said now. "One would think you didn't love me." He stroked Kyle's smooth, firm pectoral muscle. Kyle's stocky, athletic body still delighted him.

"I can't help wanting you. I wish to God I didn't."

"I'm hurt," Victor mocked.

Kyle turned to him, fire in his gray eyes. "You can't imagine what it's like. You really can't. You went from being a ruthless human to being a predator. The only difference was that now you had to attack at night. You never had to betray everything you believed, because you never believed anything."

Victor chuckled and turned on his back, clasping his hands behind his head. On the ceiling stretched the naked, brawny figure of Apollo. Victor had hired an artist to paint it there when he bought the house. "You say you can't help wanting me. But you don't love me. You can't. Can an infant truly love? Just because it cries for a teat doesn't mean it loves the mother who offers it. If you want fulfillment, you must leave the thrall's life behind. You must become like me. But that's what you fear. Once you are like me, your foolish longings will cease. You'll no longer need your God. Perhaps you'll no longer need me. But you will be free to choose. Now you content yourself with suffering. You see it as your due punishment. As if it will redeem you. It won't. So leave it. Join me."

"You don't *know* that I'll stop suffering," Kyle blurted. "What if nothing changes for me?"

"It will."

"You don't know."

"Suit yourself." Victor got up and went to the window. The

street was dark. The city had still not restored electric power to the lampposts. Perhaps he would stroll to the Quarter and find amusement in a nightclub. He took a new shirt from the enormous armoire.

"Victor," Kyle called.

Victor turned to him. Pleased when he saw the hunger in the eyes of his thrall, he smiled. He approached the bed and teased Kyle with his bare wrist, offering it, then pulling it away.

"Please!" Kyle moaned.

Victor punctured a vein with his nail. Then he lifted his wrist as though he himself would lap the drops that beaded there. A look of panic overcame Kyle at the thought of being deprived of his nourishment. Victor laughed and finally offered Kyle his wrist. He sucked the blood with relish until he was satisfied. Then he relaxed, a dreamy look on his face. Victor stroked his pale cheek, climbed out of bed, and finished dressing.

Leaving Kyle dozing in the bedroom, Victor set off down St. Charles Street toward the Quarter, a walk of a mile and a half. As his increased power—the power of a vampire maker—surged through him with every step, he thought he had never felt as young or strong or keenly alert to every scrape and buzz in the night. Even in the first year of his nocturnal existence, two millennia before, when his newly acquired powers had astounded him, he had felt uncertain of them. He had needed to learn how to wield them, as a solider equipped with a newer, more potent weapon must integrate it into his own being. His power was now as much a part of him as the air he breathed.

He could not be certain that it was a match for the Dark Kingdom. Kyle was right. Victor did not absolutely know that another transgression would not be punished. He was only sure that Kyle had begun to wear on him, as other thralls had done.

As usual, his delight in controlling his thrall began devolving into annoyance. Unless Kyle stopped groveling, he just might have to perish. Still, Victor felt affection for Kyle, and, of course, a thrall was a useful thing—especially in taking care of mundane affairs in a still disorganized city.

Yet, he would gladly trade the convenience of a thrall for the chance to test the new strength within him. What if he could create a vampire with impunity—without being forced even to separate from him, let alone to take his own place in the Dark Kingdom? The Dark Kingdom's agents were benevolent, after a fashion, determined to protect their own, even if they were also determined to uphold the order that allowed life to flow in their realm. Or so he had learned from Sonia, the agent from the Dark Kingdom who had confronted him in Georgetown four years ago. Dark-haired, fair-skinned, and buxom, looking more like a peasant than an executive of a superior realm, she had whispered in his ear, "All life is frozen in our world, until order is restored. This is the cosmic law. Our kind of dark force cannot be concentrated. Vampires cannot associate."

Hence the compromise. He had abandoned his vampire lover. The Dark Kingdom had been appeased.

But what if they had no choice? If they could not force him to take his place in the Dark Kingdom, could they really force him to separate from his vampire creation? Four years ago, he had been unwilling to risk testing the law. He had loved Paul, his vampire creation, and Sonia had threatened to take Paul's life should the transgression continue. "We love our own," she had said. "But we must preserve our own bliss, for ourselves and for those who would join us."

Their bliss. What did he care for it? And what if Sonia had been lying all the time? He would not have risked it for Paul. But for

Kyle? Certainly, he was sweet. Even comforting. But couldn't he be replaced by a hundred charming youths in New Orleans or elsewhere? Besides, Victor could not resist a play for power. As a vampire maker, he might name his own terms for stalking the earth. As he made vampire after vampire, perhaps the light of day might once again bathe him. Perhaps there were many, many secrets withheld from him by Sonia about the true fears of a kingdom where the inhabitants begrudged one who might reign as a solitary ruler, while they, for all their bliss, no longer wielded any power at all to distinguish them from one another.

Of course, his plot was in vain without his thrall's consent. A thrall might be created against his will, just as he might be destroyed against it. But being rendered a vampire was another matter. Consent was required. And from a thrall whose very nature rendered him dependent on his host, consent to be abandoned was unthinkable. And it was no use trying to trick a thrall because a requirement to understand the law was likewise built into the thrall's parasitical nature.

Still, Victor's own powers of persuasion had worked with Paul. They would eventually work with Kyle. He had no doubt.

Bourbon Street was lively. Most of the clubs were open once again, their owners returning as quickly as the authorities had permitted them to do so. In one club, a dancer in a jockstrap gyrated on a bar top, patrons waving bills at him. He knelt to allow a burly patron access to the strap and the man gleefully inserted a ten-dollar bill, groping the boy's crotch as he did so.

Victor passed an hour there, impassively observing patrons from a dark corner. Then he crossed the street to another club, where a crowd watched a music video on a wide-screen monitor above the bar. He considered seducing a boy with bleached hair and wearing a sweatshirt silk-screened with the name NEW ORLEANS SAINTS. He could lead the boy to a quiet side street and take his pleasure, along with a nice quantity of warm blood—the youth was young and healthy enough to withstand more than the average amount of siphoning. But all at once, he felt a surprising presence, a presence that had eluded him for four years now, and he lost all interest in his prey.

Involuntarily, it seemed, drawn by the presence, he exited the bar and followed Bourbon Street to St. Ann, where he turned toward Jackson Square. Outside the cathedral the presence vanished. Was he inside? Why this game? Angry and obsessed with encountering the one whose presence he felt, he turned down the alley on the side of the cathedral and walked toward the back of the building, where the statue of Christ rose in the fenced yard. Implacable, the statue raised its arms in a gesture of welcoming all sinners. Victor detected no vital energy there, the sensation he always felt when Joshu was present. He backtracked, stopping at a side door of the cathedral. Determining that no one was in sight to observe him, he exerted a bit of his supernatural strength to tug the door's bolt through the door frame and entered the dark, still church.

Votive candles glowed red and blue on tiered racks. They cast their light on the plaster form of the crucified Joshu, hanging to the side of the door. He traipsed along the transept and up the center aisle and back again. He climbed the sanctuary steps to the tabernacle and placed his hand against the golden doors. He felt nothing of Joshu within them, despite the mystical fascination they held for pious believers.

"Where are you?" he shouted at the soaring vault. The sound

of his voice reverberated in the empty church. He leapt onto the altar and shouted again, "Joshu! What are you afraid of?"

If the one Victor sought heard him, he did not answer. And Victor could hardly endure the longing within his being, so ancient by now, but always new, always surprising in its intensity. The feeling was the closest he ever felt to sheer desperation, to an understanding of what his thralls must have felt. But he possessed nothing of a sympathetic imagination, and the glimmer of understanding did not penetrate his predator's heart. And like all of his most intense feelings, this one quickly transformed itself into violent anger. He sprang to the floor and crossed the transept to the crucifix. What had the young priest said about its age? Was it an eighteenth-century creation? Very new compared to his lifetime of bearing something of the real crucifix within him. He had after all stood under the dying Jesus, the one he called Joshu, fighting the urge to lap the blood that streamed from his feet. By then, Victor had already been transformed into a vampire. And not long after the day of execution, as he stole through the dark streets of Jerusalem, he had for the first time encountered the risen Joshu.

"Victor, come to this place with me," he had said, wrapped in white burial cloths, his face shining with oil with which the women had anointed him before he was carried into the tomb hewn from the side of a stony hill.

"What place?"

"My father's house has many rooms."

"You want to confine me to a room? Will you share it with me?"

Joshu smiled placidly without answering.

"No? Then what do I care about your eternity? It's frozen and empty compared to mine. You can come back when you have a better offer."

And Joshu had come back, again and again over the centuries. Hoping to claim Victor for his eternity. But how real was Joshu's invitation? How might one travel from one realm to another? Joshu seemed confident that it might be done, that to join him in the icy pure realm he inhabited was not only possible but was the final goal of all creatures, regardless of their realms. So like a Jew, devoted to monotheism, so self-righteous and utterly blind to other spheres and other moralities. Joshu had pursued him through the centuries as much as Victor had pursued Joshu. And to what end?

Victor reached up and lifted the crucifix from the wall. It must have weighed several hundred pounds, but to one with Victor's supernatural strength it might have been a sculpture made of paper. With one thrust, he hurled it to the floor, and the corpus broke into three pieces.

3

Charles stretched in his bed, under the whirling ceiling fan. The day was warm and muggy, as many November days are in New Orleans. Morning light passed through the French doors that opened out to a courtyard balcony, or gallery, but the sun's direct rays wouldn't clear the building that fronted the gallery until almost noon. In nothing but his briefs, Charles kicked off the sheets, climbed out of bed, pulled on a plush terry cloth bathrobe, and went to the kitchen to make coffee. The trip took him through the cozy living room, furnished with rattan chairs and a sectional sofa, with scenes of Rome hanging in box frames on the walls. The gallery ran the full length of Charles's second-floor apartment in the remodeled slave quarters of the front building, once a family mansion. The archdiocese had purchased the whole property for the priests who staffed the cathedral. The old slave quarters housed Monsignor Dupree on the first floor and Charles on the second. Apartments had been created for them from several small rooms, once deemed of sufficient size for the house servants. On the third floor, the original walls divided the space into small guest rooms.

Charles carried his coffee out onto the gallery where lush ferns hung from the decorative ironwork framing the whole balcony. A fountain gurgled down in the courtyard around a statue of the Madonna. Ficuses, philodendrons, and flowering hibiscus flourished on the perimeters of the brick floor of the courtyard, and wisteria covered the walls joining the front and back buildings. A light glowed in a window of the front building, now used as the cathedral offices and reception rooms. The monsignor was an early riser. He worked in his office until it was time to walk the three blocks to the cathedral to say morning Mass each weekday. Charles took care of the weekday evening Masses.

Charles sat in an iron chair on the gallery and picked up his breviary, which he kept on a table next to it. The third-floor gallery provided a protective cover for the book, but the once gilded edges of the pages had turned pink from rain that had blown in during a bad storm. Charles made the sign of the cross and devoutly read the psalms and scripture readings. In his five months as a priest, he had never once forsaken his duty to read the Divine Office. But his faithfulness to the ritual didn't preclude distractions, and halfway through the second psalm, his mind wandered to the pale duo he'd seen last week at the All Saints' Mass. He'd thought about them frequently, especially wondering what miserable bond kept Kyle at Victor's beck and call. Kyle's strange confession about craving blood played through his mind. Had Kyle been referring to sadomasochism? During his own wild days, Charles had gone home on occasion with someone into bondage or beating. Not my thing, he'd said. I like it clean, so you decide. Usually the guy had yielded, while managing to draw Charles into a little wrestling match. But something told Charles that there was more to Kyle's dependency than conventional S & M. He'd looked for Kyle every night at Mass, but without luck. Maybe he attended morning Mass, or maybe Victor had successfully prevented him from returning to the cathedral altogether. Charles wished he could help Kyle. But he was afraid of his own motives. Was he moved by brotherly love, or by something more primal? Whenever he thought of Kyle's sweet face and compact, muscular body—the body of a soccer player—he felt breathless, his groin tingling. He was afraid that if Kyle's bare body showed up on Dr. Beauchamp's monitor, the plethysmograph would indict him. Could Christ retract his cure? If so, why would he? Had Charles done something to offend Christ? He could think of nothing. He had been faithful to prayer and dedicated to his parishioners. Maybe he'd presumed too much on God's power, not taking care to guard his eyes, to guard his thoughts. "You shalt not tempt the Lord thy God!"—thus did Christ reply to Satan, when Satan coaxed him to leap from the temple to prove that God's angels would rescue him from death.

Or were the urgings some kind of test of his trust in Christ's power to heal?

He had no answers. He only knew that the tranquility he had experienced ever since his cure was now shaken. He promised Christ to do his best to overcome his illicit feelings. He prayed for strength. Because surely Christ did not want him to abandon Kyle. *Keep me pure, O Lord.* The prayer he whispered that morning on his gallery was his frequent prayer.

When he finished praying, Charles showered and shaved. Then he donned his clerical shirt and collar and boarded his Vespa, which he kept parked in the courtyard. Two house-bound parishioners who lived in the Garden District had asked him to bring them communion. He went by the cathedral to pick up two consecrated wafers. Morning Mass would be over by now, and he could retrieve the wafers from the tabernacle without interrupting worship. He entered the open doors of the church and proceeded down the aisle to find the monsignor and the sexton crouching over something near the side door.

"My God," he said. It was the crucifix, its corpus broken into pieces. The bent legs of Christ and his midsection lay near the baptismal font. The upper body, arms, and head remained in one piece, still attached to the cross. On the wall, the dark outline of a cross indicated where the crucifix had hung.

The monsignor straightened up and shook his head. "Someone broke in through the side door," he said, nodding to the door. Dupree was a tall, stern-looking man in his fifties, with deep creases in his brow and thick salt-and-pepper hair, cropped close. "Go ahead and call the police," he said to the sexton.

The sexton, a stoop-shouldered man with snowy hair and eyebrows, nodded and disappeared into the sacristy.

"I didn't want to report this until we finished Mass," Dupree explained.

Incredulous, Charles shook his head and let out a long whistle. "This is crazy. Why would someone do it? You think they planned to steal it? Is anything missing?"

"Not from what I can tell. And it doesn't look like they planned to steal it. It looks like they destroyed it on purpose. Like they threw it down."

"Then there must have been two or three guys. This thing must weigh a ton."

"The city has gone to the dogs!" the monsignor said in disgust. Then he sighed. "Of course, the police won't do a thing about this. Not with a whole city still in shambles."

"It looks like it can be repaired," Charles said to console him.

"Let's pray to God it can. For the sake of the parishioners. Mrs. Benette left Mass in tears."

Charles nodded, sickened by the sight of the broken corpus. It was as if Christ himself had been mutilated. But he had to shake off his revulsion and attend to his pastoral duties. So he retrieved the consecrated wafers from the tabernacle and secured them in a pyx, round and gold as an old-fashioned pocket watch.

He went outside and boarded the Vespa. He whizzed along Royal Street, which turned into St. Charles on the other side of Canal Street. Many of the Royal Street antique and art shops were open again for business. And tourists strolled along the street, peering in the plate-glass windows. Traffic was fairly light on Canal, a busy thoroughfare before the hurricane. Windows here and there in stores and hotels along the street were still boarded from looting after the storm.

By the time he reached the first parishioner's Georgian mansion, big drops of rain struck his helmet. He hurried to the door and rang the bell. An elderly woman appeared at the door and welcomed him into the house. He stayed with her until the storm subsided and then headed to the house of a wheelchair-bound parishioner, whose brother had drowned in the hurricane. A thin, timid woman in scrubs met him at the front door of the large house and led him to a sunroom in back of the house, which had been turned into a bedroom since the upper story was inaccessible to the man. Charles greeted the old parishioner in the wheelchair and sat down on the bed near him. The old man wasted little time in recounting the recent tragedy of his brother's death.

"He went to the attic, Father," the man said, his rheumy blue eyes filling. "The water kept rising in the house, and so he went up there. He must have thought it couldn't rise any higher. But it did. He couldn't get out. He didn't have anything up there to break through the roof."

"That's horrible, Mr. Lanier." He touched Mr. Lanier's veinous hand to comfort him.

"Why did God let it happen?" the old man said.

Charles shrugged and shook his head. "I don't know. But he's with God now. God was with him then."

"He was the only brother I had left. The rest are dead. They've all gone." The old man choked out the last words, close to sobbing.

"Let's pray for him," Charles suggested. He pulled his rosary out of his pocket. "Can we do that?"

The old man nodded his head without answering, and he followed Charles's lead as the priest made the sign of the cross. They prayed the rosary, softly, the old man choking up from time to time. When they finished, Charles blessed him. He rose to go when the thin health care worker arrived to help the old man with his meds.

Outside, he boarded the Vespa and took off. When he turned down First Avenue, he noticed someone opening the gate to a mansion hidden behind a vine-covered wall and tall magnolias. He recognized Kyle. He was dressed in blue jeans and a red knit shirt. By the time Charles called to him, it was too late. Kyle had disappeared behind the wall. Charles pulled up on the sidewalk and peered through the gates just as the front door of the Greek Revival mansion closed. The drapes were drawn over the windows. He looked for a bell to ring or a speaker to buzz, but there were none near the gate. So much for visitors. No wonder Kyle seemed miserable, immured inside the mansion, chained to Victor.

He considered waiting there for Kyle to reemerge. But when might that be? And what would Charles say to him, anyway? He lingered, reluctant to leave. But finally he gave up, heading down the street with a strong sense of foreboding rising in him. He felt that Kyle was in danger, spiritual and physical. Twice, he stopped and considered going back. But what could he do? He couldn't break down the gate. He couldn't call the police and tell them that Kyle was under the power of his companion. He finally returned to the Quarter.

That night, he tossed and turned in bed. At two thirty, he'd barely fallen asleep when his alarm went off. He got up and fumbled for his clothes. He'd signed up for the three o'clock Holy Hour at the cathedral. On Fridays the Blessed Sacrament was displayed in an ornate monstrance on the altar, and parishioners took turns keeping vigil before it, praying for the rebuilding of the city and the return of all the evacuees to the abandoned neighborhoods on low ground. For the devastated Ninth Ward, nothing short of a miracle could make that happen.

When he reached the dark cathedral, the monstrance rose on the altar between two glowing candelabra. Charles found the young sentinel nodding off in the first pew. He squeezed the boy's shoulder, sent him on his way, then knelt and crossed himself. He prayed for Kyle, that he could escape Victor, that he could find happiness. And he prayed for himself, that his motives would be pure.

He had been kneeling for ten minutes, when the side door opened and someone entered. He assumed that it was one of the men in the parish who sometimes joined him in his nocturnal adoration. He waited for the man to emerge from the shadows. But for a long time, no one appeared. Finally a man in a cassock and Roman collar crossed the transept and climbed the sanctuary steps to the altar. Who could this be? The only priests at the cathedral were the monsignor and himself. Why would a strange priest, and one dressed so formally, show up now?

The priest knelt on the floor directly in front of the

monstrance. Suddenly the flames of the candelabra swelled as though a jet of gas rushed through them. Charles started at the sight, which he'd barely absorbed when the whole altar suddenly burst into flames. Instantly, Charles shot to his feet, astounded.

"Get away from there!" he shouted to the man. Had someone poured fuel on the altar? What had caused it to suddenly ignite? These questions barely penetrated Charles's consciousness, he was so alarmed about the priest. But the man remained transfixed, despite Charles's cries. Finally, braving the flames, Charles approached the man to pull him away. He felt the heat from the blaze on his face and hands as he grabbed the man's arm. "Come on," he shouted.

The face that turned to look at him belonged to Kyle. His gray wolf-eyes were wild in the light of the fire.

"Kyle," Charles shouted, frightened by the expression. "What are you doing?"

Kyle glared at Charles, finally jerking his arm away from Charles's hold. He stood up and reached for the burning monstrance.

"Jesus!" Charles shouted, falling back. "Don't touch it!"

Kyle could not be stopped. He hugged the fiercely hot, gleaming vessel to his face, kissing the wafer displayed in the round window at the center of the monstrance, oblivious to the fire around him. A red liquid streamed from the vessel, as though the sacred host, the body of Christ, oozed blood. The blood smeared Kyle's face and dripped down his hands. He lowered the vessel, and a look of horror came over him. "In the name of Christ, help me!" he screamed to Charles.

Despite his fear, Charles reached to pull him from the flames. But in an instant, the blaze was suddenly extinguished—as though the air had been sucked from the room. Kyle, who had been as vivid, as real as his own flesh and blood, suddenly vanished. Confused, Charles turned and searched the shadowy church for a hint of movement behind a pillar or in one of the alcoves. But there was no sign of Kyle.

Charles's attention returned to the dark sanctuary. There was no more heat. No more conflagration. Not even a scorch mark on the altar cloth. It was perfectly intact. The monstrance once again rested quietly on the altar, flanked by soft candlelight, no sign that it had ever been disturbed.

Stunned, his heart pounding, Charles sat on marble floor of the sanctuary, staring at the tranquil altar. What had he just witnessed? The scene before him had been as real as his own flesh. He'd felt the heat. He'd felt Kyle. He couldn't have dreamed it. And yet . . . a real fire would have left traces—the acrid smell of fuel, soot on the monstrance, a charred altar cloth. Maybe the fire was some kind of apparition, like the apparition of Christ, four years ago. The experience had the same intensity as that apparition. But then, he'd been cured. What could be the point of this apparition? Why had Kyle been in it? Why had he been dressed like a priest?

He got up and ventured to touch the altar. It was as cool as the wall of a cave. No scorch marks anywhere. No smell of fire in the air. Not one sign that an inferno had just been raging in St. Louis Cathedral.

"Hey," Charles whispered to the monstrance. "I'm no good at figuring out these things. Can you give me a clue?"

The only response was silence.

Weak now, exhausted and weak, Charles returned to the pew and sat, leaning forward, his elbows on his knees, trying to understand. Was God telling him to help Kyle, no matter what his own feelings for Kyle might be? Surely, God would not call attention to Kyle's torment and expect Charles to remain aloof? But if he was supposed to rescue Kyle, how would he accomplish that? The vision offered no clues. And what if Kyle didn't really want to be saved from whatever perverse dependency he had on Victor? Then what? How was Charles supposed to rip him from Victor's clutches?

Charles slept little that night. The next morning, he rode to the Garden District and watched the mansion for over an hour with no sign of Kyle. When an elderly neighbor emerged from the Federal style mansion across the street, Charles told the woman who he was and that he was trying to contact Kyle. He told a white lie to reassure her. He said that Kyle was a parishioner of his. She had no reason not to believe him. He wore his Roman collar, and his good nature and good looks had the usual effect on her.

"I've never met the people who live there," she said, buttoning her gray cardigan despite the warm, muggy air. "They come and go quietly. Did they evacuate during Katrina?"

"I don't know."

"Well, if they didn't, I'm glad. There was no looting around here. Maybe they kept an eye on things." As the woman spoke, a drop of blood suddenly fell from her nose onto her sweater, followed by another, and another. "Oh, my!" she said, cupping her spotted hands beneath her nose.

"Put pressure on it," Charles said, concerned for her.

She squeezed her nostrils, turned abruptly without a sign of dismissal, and started back toward her house. As she made her way, the wind suddenly picked up, gusting in stormlike blasts. All around, the branches were shaking fiercely. Where had the storm come from all at once? The frail woman fought the force, which blew the sweater from her shoulders. Charles retrieved it for her and helped her to her door. Once she was inside, the air turned calm again. Charles stared at the mansion across the street with dread, feeling that somehow, as impossible as it seemed, the owner was responsible for the sudden storm.

Finally, Charles realized there was nothing he could do. He couldn't break into the house if he'd wanted to. Feeling helpless, he went home, but all day he was haunted by the previous night's vision in the cathedral and by the weird storm in the Garden District in the morning.

That evening after the five o'clock Mass, he returned to the Garden District and positioned himself behind the sagging branches of a magnolia across the street from Kyle and Victor's dwelling. Victor suddenly appeared just outside the gate, though Charles had not seen him approaching it. Victor hesitated before turning the key, cocking his head as though he listened for a noise. Then the iron gate squealed open and clanged shut behind him. Victor climbed the porch steps and entered the house.

Charles crossed the street and peered through the bars. The drapes on the first floor were open, and lamps glowed in the house. Victor passed before the window, standing in profile. He wore a black turtleneck, and his face seemed alabaster against it. For a split second, Charles imagined that Victor turned and stared at him with red, demonic eyes and with his canines bared, as he had imagined them to be bared that day in the cathedral. He shivered and stepped back from the gate. He had the urge to call out to Kyle, to beat on the gates until Victor opened them. But before he could act on it, a sense of disorientation overcame him. He felt himself falling. He seemed to feel the damp ground beneath his fingers. He lost consciousness.

When he awoke it was dark. But he was no longer outside. He was in his own bed, the fan spinning overhead. He felt drugged. His head throbbed. What had happened? Had Victor attacked him. If so, how? Before blacking out, he'd seen Victor moving inside the house, nowhere near him. Maybe someone else had attacked him. But why? To rob him? He felt for his wallet in his hip pocket. Switching on the lamp, he inspected the wallet. His credit card was still there. So was a twenty dollar bill.

And how had he ended up back in his room? Maybe Kyle had seen the attack or had come upon him afterward and got help to carry him home. Nothing made sense.

He got up and took something for the headache and glanced outside to see if his Vespa was in the courtyard. It was there, parked beside the wall. He had no memory of riding it home. Could Kyle have retrieved it for him?

Too exhausted to think anymore about it, he climbed back into bed and fell deeply asleep.

Every day for a week, Charles returned to his post outside the mansion. He wanted answers. Was Kyle all right? Was there an explanation for the attack on Charles? He was willing to risk his own safety to find out the truth, but he observed caution. He restricted his watch to the daylight hours. Whatever had caused his blackout had something to do with Victor, and he had no intention of provoking Kyle's tormentor. He'd never feared anyone the way he feared Victor. Maybe it was the man's act of sacrilege in the cathedral. Maybe it was the preternatural look he had seen in Victor's gaze, and the canines that kept flashing before his mind's eye.

Whatever it was, he sensed that Victor was pure evil. What else explained his intense determination to take advantage of Kyle's obvious vulnerability? The worst kind of vulnerability. If Charles had learned anything since his cure, it was that God willed people to be whole and only one thing could guarantee that: knowing your belovedness, knowing that no one and nothing could control your destiny, because you belonged to God. This truth was lost on Kyle, and Victor exploited Kyle's ignorance. Victor was ignorant of the truth too, but his ignorance took the form of pride and malice. They loomed in his soul like vicious predators, and they'd made him a predator, too.

During his vigils, Charles did not catch so much as a glimpse of Kyle. Of course, it was possible that Kyle came and went when Charles was not keeping watch. Still, he'd begun to consider calling the police to report his suspicion that Kyle was in danger, when Kyle finally came to him. It was during evening Mass. Charles watched him enter the church and kneel in a back pew. When it came time for communion, Kyle did not join the line that formed down the central aisle. He knelt with his face buried in his hands. After the final benediction, Charles quickly removed his vestments in the sacristy and hurried out. He was afraid Kyle might have rushed back out into the night. But he was still there, kneeling in the pew. As Charles advanced toward the back of the church, a woman leaving a pew stopped him.

"Father, I wanted to tell you about my brother's family." She clung to his arm. She was a short woman, in her sixties. Her dyed blond hair was bobbed.

Worried that Kyle would get away, Charles was tempted to shake himself free from her. But when he glanced at Kyle's pew, he found Kyle still kneeling. So he turned his attention back to the woman.

"They evacuated the city. Went to Houston. They still can't return to Lakeside. It just makes me sick. Please pray for them. I don't know what I'll do without him. He's been a rock for me, ever since my husband died."

As Charles listened sympathetically to her, his eyes wandered over to Kyle, who suddenly got up to leave.

Charles panicked. "I'm sorry," he said, pulling away from the woman. "I have to speak to someone." Charles left her, hurrying after Kyle, but by the time he stepped outside the cathedral, Kyle was nowhere in sight. He seemed to have disappeared into thin air.

Charles approached a tarot card reader who had set up her table in the paved area in front of the church, and asked her if she'd seen where Kyle had gone.

"The guy who was crying?" she said. She wore heavy mascara and hoop earrings. "He went that way." She motioned toward the river with a pudgy hand.

Charles darted away, running along Jackson Square to Decatur Street. A few tourists inspected an artist's paintings on the sidewalk in front of the square. Two horses and their carriages stood nearby, the tour guides in the driver's seats hoping for customers from the scant crowd of tourists seated at tables across the street at Café Du Monde. But there was no sign of Kyle. Where could he have gone? Charles crossed Decatur, looking up and down the street in vain, then mounted the concrete stairs that led to the promenade along the river. The night was damp and chilly. A barge made its slow way along the current. The town of Algiers lay dimly lit on the opposite bank.

Down the promenade, still dark after the hurricane, the silhouette of a man hovered near the water's edge, as if he considered jumping into the river. Charles recognized Kyle. He did not call out for fear of precipitating a desperate move. Instead he walked quietly along the river until he was barely ten feet from Kyle. Then he softly spoke his name.

"Leave me alone," Kyle answered.

"Come and sit down on this bench," Charles coaxed, forcing himself to keep his voice calm and bring Kyle back to reason.

"It's no use."

"You don't believe that. Why else would you come to the cathedral?"

"To ask forgiveness."

"You have that. No matter what. So why try to hurt yourself?"

Kyle let out an incredulous laugh. "If you only knew."

"Then tell me." Charles ventured a step toward Kyle.

"You wouldn't believe me. You would *never* believe me." He threw a sidelong glance at Charles. "I'm not crazy."

"No," Charles said. "You're just desperate. Look, why don't we go to my place and talk? It's quiet. I've got all night." Nervous sweat streamed down Charles's sides. *Please, God*, he said to himself. *Make him listen.*

"You won't believe me," Kyle repeated.

"I'll do my best. I know you're not crazy." Charles slowly approached Kyle and touched his shoulder. "Please."

Kyle pulled away, and Charles was ready to grab him and force him away from the river when suddenly Kyle went limp. He trembled and started crying. Charles embraced him, wrapping his arms around him. Finally Kyle allowed himself to be led away, and the pair walked quietly back into the Quarter. An occasional streetlamp glowed on the dormers and galleries and narrow streets, where the nineteenth-century structures varied from seedy to charming. Twice, Kyle stopped, appearing to listen for something. But the only sound was the low horn of a barge moaning on the river. Charles glanced around nervously, too. He believed he knew what Kyle feared, and he understood the fear. Victor on the prowl, determined to force his protégé to go back with him.

On Dumaine, Charles unlocked the gate to his home and led Kyle through the narrow mews that ran along the side of the front mansion. They walked through the courtyard and up the stairs to his apartment. In the stillness of the damp night, the ferns on the gallery hung motionless, like deformed stalactites.

Inside, Charles switched on a table lamp and led Kyle to the sectional sofa. "Sit down. I'll get you something to drink."

"No. I don't want anything." Kyle sat down.

Charles sat across from him in a rattan chair.

"I want to start from the beginning," Kyle said. He seemed in control now, fixed in his intention, a note of fatalism in his voice, as though he might as well explain everything before the world came crashing down.

"All right," Charles said, settling back in his chair.

Kyle took a breath and let it out slowly. He unzipped his light jacket, revealing a pale blue T-shirt. There were rusty drops on it. At first, Charles thought they must be drops of paint. But on closer inspection they looked like bloodstains. Was Kyle wounded? Charles searched his face. He found no sign of a wound on the pale flesh. But Kyle's eyes were full of pain.

4

I was a priest," Kyle began. "In the Archdiocese of Washington."

Charles started at the remark, remembering his vision.

"You're surprised?"

Charles shook his head. "It's just that I had a kind of . . . a feeling you were a priest."

"It's what I'd always lived for. I was the associate pastor at St. Ignatius Church in the District. It was in a pretty run-down neighborhood. Lots of drugs. Lots of shootings. But some sweet kids. I started a neighborhood basketball team. We played against other neighborhood teams. The church operated a soup kitchen in the basement. I was in my element. You know what I mean?" Kyle beamed, and he removed his jacket, as though he was more comfortable now. "The life I always wanted. Close to God. A shepherd for God's people."

"I know the feeling." Charles smiled. Even though the life of a pastor was new to him, he was already sure that it suited him perfectly.

"There's nothing like it," Kyle said, his voice full of regret. "Anyway, the pastor had some heart problems. He was replaced by another priest named Gimello. Gimello was a by-the-book guy.

Strict. Devout. I thought he was a saint. He looked like I imagined the Dominicans must have looked in Spain during the Inquisition. Dark hair, pulled back in a ponytail. A goatee. Black eyes that could look right through you. At first, I was happy he came. I thought we'd pray together, discuss spiritual treatises."

"That didn't happen?" Charles said, happy that Kyle was opening up to him.

"Oh, it did happen. Gimello laid out a fasting regimen. And once a week, we kept vigil the whole night before the Blessed Sacrament. One reason I was grateful for his discipline was my own temptations." Kyle lowered his eyes in shame.

"Against purity?" Charles guessed.

"I thought I'd overcome them. During my seminary days, my spiritual director helped me. I stuck to the straight and narrow. Then after ordination, with all the excitement of parish life— saying Mass, hearing confession, consoling grieving people, marrying couples. With all of that, who has time for temptations?"

The topic caused Charles discomfort. It struck too close to home because of his attraction to Kyle.

"What more could anyone want. Right?" Kyle continued. "Well, that's what I thought. Then Gimello launched a campaign against a man who he said was desecrating a church in Georgetown. The man had turned it into a private club for people who practiced the occult and sadomasochism. Sexual perversion was the worst sin, Gimello said. It was the only unforgiveable sin. Because it is a defilement of the body, which is the temple of the Holy Spirit."

"Come on!" Charles objected. "What about genocide? What about exploitation and corruption?"

"I'm just telling you what he believed. And what I believed."

"Believed? You don't believe it now?"

Kyle stared gravely at him, his face as livid as milk. "Now I know something worse."

"Go on," Charles said, half curious, half afraid.

Kyle continued. "We went to the man and confronted him. That's when everything began. The man was Victor." Kyle spoke Victor's name tenderly.

"You fell in love with him?"

Kyle shook his head. "God, no. Not at first. He scared me. I thought he was evil. The things I saw in that place. A church! On the stage, the performers were . . . they were obscene. So were the people in the club. If they acted like that in public, well, I knew what kinds of things they must have done in their own rooms."

"But you were attracted to Victor all the same." Charles could see the truth in Kyle's face.

"From the beginning, he had some kind of power over me. I didn't understand it. I dreamed about him. I imagined seeing him at Mass, leering at me as I raised the host during the consecration. He got into my thoughts, and I'd suddenly find myself on his doorstep. I had no memory of going to his house, but there I was. I wanted to ring the bell, but somehow I resisted the urge and turned away. Then, one night as I prayed in the sanctuary at St. Ignatius, my arms stretched out like Jesus's arms on the cross, he was suddenly there, behind me."

"The church was unlocked?"

"No. The doors were locked."

Thunder had begun to rumble and wind to gust. Both Charles and Kyle had registered it on the periphery of their consciousness, but now a sudden crash brought the storm to their full attention. They both jumped. With a second explosion, the lights flickered and went out.

"I'll light a candle," Charles said. He went to the kitchen for matches and lit a candle in a terra-cotta holder on the coffee table. Through the French doors they could see the rain falling in torrents. Lightning flashed and thunder rumbled at regular intervals.

Kyle gazed apprehensively at the windows.

"Don't worry," Charles said. "He doesn't know where you are."

Kyle's half-smile suggested that Charles spoke naively. "He always knows. Like that night. Suddenly he was behind me. Then he had me in his arms. And I couldn't resist. For all of my prayer and fasting and discipline. I couldn't resist him. And there on the floor of the sanctuary . . ." Kyle hesitated, scrutinizing Charles's face, to see if he was judging him.

"You gave in to temptation," Charles said sympathetically, finishing the painful confession for Kyle.

Kyle shook his head. "It's not what you think. This is the hard truth, Father Charles. Victor pinned back my arms and I felt his mouth on my throat and then a stab and he started to siphon blood from me. A couple of warm drops fell down my neck or I wouldn't have believed it. My own blood, Father. And Victor was swallowing. Afterwards he told me that this wasn't the first time. It was only the first time I had stayed conscious. Because he willed me to stay conscious."

"What are you saying?" Charles said, shocked by Kyle's story. "Are you telling me that Victor is some kind of sick pervert?"

"No. I'm telling you exactly what it sounds like. He's a vampire."

Charles stared at him fearfully without saying a word. Maybe Kyle was more unbalanced than he had thought. A streak of lightning lit up the room. Then a crash of thunder rattled the windows.

"I'm not crazy, Father. You said so yourself. Here, look." Kyle got up and knelt by the coffee table. He raised the candle to his face. "Look at my eyes. Have you ever seen anything like them?" The pupils of Kyle's eyes shrank as he raised the light to them and seemed to scintillate as though a current passed through them. His skin glowed like white fabric under a black light. "And feel my hand." He reached out across the table.

Charles touched the extended palm. It was cool as raw meat. Charles recoiled, jerking his own hand away. "You're saying he made you what he is?"

Kyle shook his head. "After he finished with me, he tore his wrist with his teeth and forced my mouth to the wound. He told me to drink. He had me by the back of the neck. His grip was like a vise. So what could I do? That's when I changed—not to what he is. I'm not free the way he is. I'm in limbo. I'm not what he is and I'm not what I used to be. What you are. I'm his thrall. I exist for his pleasure. Are you taking this in? You wanna hear more?"

Charles was thinking of his vision of Kyle in the cathedral. He remembered Kyle's plea: *In the name of Christ, help me!* Whatever he was saying—incredible as it was—he needed help now.

Kyle took Charles's silence as permission to continue. "Everything changed for me. My senses got so sharp, it hurt to look at bright colors. I could smell wild animals and rodents, too, from a distance—raccoons in the sewers, and rats. My fingernails started growing like this." He held the candle to his hand and displayed nails that were two inches long. "I trim them every morning, and by evening they've grown back." Kyle returned to the sofa, but even at this distance from the candle his face and hands were preternaturally white and vivid.

"I lost everything I ever cared about," he continued. "My family.

The priesthood. The priesthood! When I see you behind the altar, doing what I prepared to do for my whole life, I want to die. I've even lost Christ."

"You can never lose Christ," Charles blurted adamantly. Despite his confusion about how to respond to this morbid, incredible confession, he knew how to respond to this.

"Never?" Kyle said. "I know I want to believe that as I sit there in church. I can't stay away. No matter what Victor does to me. But if you knew everything that I know—if you believed me now, you'd see it a different way."

"No I wouldn't!" Charles insisted.

"There's no way to pass from here to there!" Kyle shouted, suddenly angry.

Charles refused to back down, for Kyle's good and for his own. "Isn't that what you were trying to do by the river?"

"You know better than that. No one who commits suicide is saved."

"I don't believe that!" Charles refused to believe that God condemned someone to hell for all eternity for an act of desperation.

Kyle shrugged as though it made no difference what Charles believed.

"Then why did you want to hurt yourself?"

"I just want it to be over. If I go to hell, then at least I'm free from him. And from myself. At least then I'd be where God wants me to be. But, I don't believe I'll go there. Not even to hell. I belong to this sphere now."

Spellbound, Charles listened as Kyle explained the nature of the Dark Kingdom—at least, as much of it as Victor had explained to Kyle. As he watched Kyle's livid face in the darkness and heard the young man's words amid the drumming rain—words as strangely coherent as they were desperate—he could not help believing there must be some kind of truth in what Kyle said. He spoke with conviction. He wasn't deranged.

It was after two in the morning when Kyle finished.

"That's all I know," Kyle said. "It doesn't matter whether you believe me or not. Victor will know that I told you."

"What will he do?" Charles said, scared for him.

"He'll say this proves that I should become what he is. Or I'll never stop being tortured."

"Become a vampire? Then he'll go to that place. The Dark Kingdom." Charles was surprised that he referred to this place as though he believed in it completely. But how could he?

"Maybe not." Kyle stood up. "I have to go."

Charles got up too. "Why don't you stay here tonight? There are guest rooms on the third floor." The words were out of his mouth before he could stop them. But surely he had no ulterior motives. Surely he wanted only to keep Kyle safe.

Kyle shook his head. "He'll come for me. I'm surprised he hasn't come yet."

"He can't make you do anything!"

"Haven't you heard a thing I've said? You do think I'm crazy. Don't you?"

"No. I don't. I mean, I don't know what I believe. It's just a lot to take in." Charles wanted more than anything to reassure Kyle that he believed he was sane, no matter how distraught or confused. He wanted Kyle to know that he could understand something of his anguish. "Listen," he said. "I have something to tell you. I can understand your feelings, about other men."

Kyle threw him a belligerent look. "So that's why you want me to stay tonight. That's why you listened to all of this."

"What?" At first Charles was confused. Then he realized what Kyle was implying and felt his face get warm. "Hell no. That's not true. Look, I've been celibate for four years, and I won't throw that out."

"Then why did you tell me?"

Charles shrugged, fumbling for words. "I don't know. You opened up to me. I guess I just wanted to do the same."

Kyle nodded, satisfied. "So, you've kept your vow of celibacy," he said enviously. "For me, it was always a battle. My Achilles heel. That's why I am where I am."

"I don't believe there's no hope for you." Charles grabbed Kyle by the arm and looked into his gray eyes.

Those eyes had been so intense, so serious up to this point. Now they revealed a hint of wistfulness, as though Kyle longed to believe what Charles was saying. "You don't know the evil I've seen. My life is darker than you could ever imagine."

"You don't have a corner on the market," Charles shot back. "Evil is everywhere. Goodness is just stronger. I'm telling you from my own experience. I had attractions to men. I even gave in to them. Now they're gone. God cured me."

Kyle snorted, indignantly.

"It's true," Charles said. Then, realizing how he must sound, self-righteous and judgmental, he apologized. "I'm not judging you. I'm trying to say I understand. If Christ hadn't had mercy on me, I don't know where I'd be." A wave of anxiety rose in him as he boasted of the cure he'd now begun to doubt.

Kyle seemed unconvinced by the declaration, but he didn't argue. His concerns clearly lay elsewhere. "Meet me in a few hours at Lafayette Cemetery. At eleven thirty. They lock the gates at noon. Then we'll see if you still believe what you're saying."

Kyle left just as the wind and rain picked up. From the gallery, Charles watched him pass through the wet courtyard and disappear into the shadows of the little mews that led to the gate on the street.

For a long time, Charles lay awake in his bed, still seeing Kyle's livid face, long nails, and strange, scintillating pupils. He replayed in his mind the scene Kyle had described: Victor pinning Kyle to the floor of the sanctuary to feed on the young man's throat, blood trailing down his fierce face, then tearing open his wrist for Kyle to drink. Charles replayed Kyle's words about the transformation of his senses, and he imagined dark alleys and quiet streets where Victor stalked unsuspecting victims. He imagined Lafayette Cemetery in the dark, where Victor's form wandered through the tombs and drooping branches. According to lore, graveyards were the resting places of vampires. Isn't that why Kyle wanted to meet at Lafayette? To take him to Victor's resting place? He shivered at the thought—even though their meeting would take place in daylight. Now in the dark room, in the dark, damp Quarter, Charles, who rarely lost a night of sleep over anything, felt full of apprehension. When he finally drifted off, he dreamed of Victor. The man was glaring up at the crucifix in the cathedral. Suddenly he bared his dangerous canines and ripped the corpus from the cross. It was no longer plaster, but bleeding flesh. Then as he pounced on the vulnerable throat of the bloody Christ, he recoiled inexplicably, crying out as though he were the last man remaining on the face of the earth, before rising, his face smeared in blood and his eyes full of horrible malice.

Charles's own eyes opened. Instantly he was aware of someone skulking in the room. He flew out of his bed, his fists up, ready to defend himself. But he found no one in the shadows. And when lightning flashed it revealed nothing but his own image in the mirror.

The rain had ceased when Charles locked up the Vespa outside of Layfayette's gates, but the sky remained overcast. On the ride there, he'd been in a daze, not thinking about how creepy it was to be meeting someone in the cemetery. Now the location finally registered in his mind. He was at a graveyard to see . . . to see what? What kind of proof could Kyle produce except the standard proof of the undead, according to ghoulish films? A corpse that wasn't a corpse. This was freakish stuff. But he felt compelled to know more, if not about Victor's nature, then about Kyle himself. He couldn't deny the tenderness he felt for Kyle. He wanted to hold him, if only to reassure him. He'd never met someone so guilt ridden, and as far as he was concerned, God hated anyone to be eaten up by guilt.

He found Kyle waiting for him just inside the cemetery, near a decrepit mausoleum whose shelves were exposed—probably a neglected family tomb. Kyle's flesh was still as white as chalk, but the eerily iridescent quality of his skin had vanished in the daylight.

"This way," he said.

He led Charles down one tomb-crowded lane and up another, to a lateral wall of the cemetery, stopping at an enormous vine-covered mausoleum with an iron door between two sets of tombs, stacked one on top of the other—judging from the engraved tablets. On the pediment was inscribed the family name: Boudreaux. Kyle scanned the lane and, detecting no one in the still, humid morning, inserted a key in the lock and opened the rusty gate.

"Go on," he said, motioning for Charles to enter first.

Charles hesitated.

"Don't worry," Kyle said. "I'm not going to lock you in."

Charles proceeded in and Kyle followed, pulling the door shut behind him. Not a dot of light penetrated the close tomb, and Charles's heart quickened its pace. He heard Kyle fumbling for something, and then a beam suddenly shone in his face.

Charles shielded his eyes.

"Sorry." Kyle directed the flashlight away from Charles and toward the stack of tombs on one side of the mausoleum. "These are empty," he said. Then he moved it to the opposite side, where a mahogany coffin rested on a waist-high shelf. The other shelves had evidently been removed.

"Are you ready?" Kyle said.

"I don't know." Charles's heart was pounding.

"You'll never believe me if you don't see."

"I'm not sure I want to believe you. And isn't it dangerous?"

"No," Kyle said. "It's noon. The sun's at its zenith. A vampire's power is never more compromised."

"But when he rises . . ." Charles could hardly believe he'd spoken such words. But in this dark tomb, standing with someone who seemed as sane as he did oppressed, Charles knew he'd entered an alternative world. And he believed in worlds not visible to most.

"He won't remember a thing. He's too weak to be conscious."

"And the daylight won't harm him?"

"Not in here. Not while he's in the coffin."

"Just get it over with."

Kyle clicked off the light.

"What are you doing?" Charles said.

"The light will disturb his sleep. Don't worry. You'll be able to see without it."

The sounds of a latch giving way and lid rising were followed by the appearance of a face as iridescent as Kyle's had been in the darkness. It was almost as though the handsome face had been painted white, contrasting dramatically with the black brows, shock of black hair, and blue-black stubble. Victor's silk shirt, opened to reveal his pale, hirsute chest, was red as blood. His white hands, big and powerful, lay quietly on the red fabric. There was no discernible movement of his chest.

"Is he breathing?" Charles whispered fearfully.

"He doesn't need to breathe when he's in his resting place. His heart is still, too. Go ahead, feel his pulse."

Reluctantly, Charles reached for Victor, clasping his wrist and quickly releasing it. "He's like ice!" He glanced at Kyle in horror before taking up the wrist again and holding it long enough to see that Kyle told the truth. There was no pulse. By all accounts, he was certifiably dead. But as he returned Victor's hand to its position, Victor's eyes flashed open. Charles jumped back, but in an instant Victor had sat up and gripped him by the throat. Unable to breathe, Charles tore at Victor's hand, but he might as well have tried to free himself from an iron trap for a jungle animal as from the powerful hand.

Kyle tried to pry him loose. "Let him go. Please! You can't kill him here! You can't."

Victor's grip relaxed. He expelled a whooshing sound through his mouth, like the sound Charles heard that corpses make on the embalming table. Victor lay down again, his face tranquil, though his mouth was open and his deadly fangs protruded from it.

Kyle closed the lid, leaving them once again in darkness.

Charles leaned against the walled tombs, rubbing his throat and struggling to catch his breath.

"I don't know how this could happen," Kyle said, shaken. "Are you all right?"

"Let's get out of here." Charles barely choked out the words.

Kyle eased open the gate enough to make sure no one stirred outside the mausoleum. Then he exited, with Charles close on his heels, locking the gate behind them.

"Come on," Kyle said. "They'll be locking the cemetery in a minute."

Silent, they moved through the tombs, the magnolia branches shuddering around them in the wind. They exited the cemetery gates and stopped on the sidewalk. Charles sank against the brick wall, still in shock.

"You believe me now," Kyle said.

Pale and solemn, Charles stared at Kyle, the horrible, incredible truth now clear to him.

5

Over the past four years, Victor had told Kyle everything about Joshu. Why should he withhold anything from him? And why shouldn't he indulge his own whims to recount those feverous years in Jerusalem? There he first encountered the captivating Jewish youth dancing in ecstasy on a cliff above Jerusalem, dancing naked for his God, he had told Victor—dancing without a trace of self-consciousness, as King David had danced before the Ark of the Covenant. This boy had stolen his heart while withholding what Victor needed from him. And Victor, who always took without asking from slave girls and subjects and even officers in the Roman legion, could not take what he wanted from Joshu. Because he wanted nothing less than passionate devotion, and that, he discovered, could only be received, not taken. Joshu's devotion belonged to the God of the Jews. "My mission has no place for you," he had said, "not in the way you want."

Overcome with fury, Victor had gone too far. Beating slaves and abusing ruffians was the prerogative of the occupying force, within limits, but Victor had spoiled the son of a respected Jewish elder and finally murdered an officer, and Pilate had called for his apprehension. Now a fugitive, Victor had accepted the offer of the one who would initiate him into the realm of the Dark

Kingdom: Tiresia, a magnificent Ethiopian beauty, full of arcane knowledge. As he drank blood from her breast, she transferred her kind of life to him and took her place in the realm she had shown him in a vision: a new Rome where feasting, games, and erotic rapture continued forever for those who had stalked the earthly night for at least two hundred years.

But ascending to the Dark Kingdom was no easy matter. It required replacing oneself with another vampire, and to accomplish that task one had to convince a human being to consent to a horrifying transformation. Likely candidates—the cruel, the violent, the power-hungry—were not the sort Victor wanted as a lover who would one day join him forever in the Dark Kingdom. Although such a replacement was not required by the Dark Kingdom's laws, it was required by Victor. He would be satisfied with nothing less than a lover who could obliterate his obsession for Joshu, which had never died, having been nurtured by regular apparitions of Joshu through the years—Joshu declaring his love, Joshu speaking of salvation—as if a being like Victor could cross the great abyss between cosmic spheres. In certain moments, Joshu's face haunted him like a lover who, only days before, had slipped from his fingers into the sea.

Victor's obsession for Joshu eventually led him to the door of one of the first monasteries in fourth-century Alexandria. In the cloister, Victor could enjoy a keen sense of Joshu's presence while at the same time striking out against the God who had stolen Joshu from him. Assuming the role of a monk—and feigning a disease that made him intolerant of sunlight—he slept by day within the cloister's crypt and arose at night to prey on villagers and even on the monks themselves. Over the centuries, he repeated this ruse again and again, moving from cloister to unsuspecting cloister.

It had been gratifying to lie among the bones of monks whose piety won them a place in Joshu's heaven. In heaven, he believed, they knelt like statues before the throne of the Lamb, their frozen souls nevermore capable of vitality and passion. The fools deserved their punishment. Brutes of his kind could look forward to a far different heaven, full of erotic rapture for superior beings who, under a moon bright as a silver sun, became more themselves than they had been in their existence beneath a moon destined to wane. Brutes of his kind could look forward to that when they were ready.

Would Victor ever be ready? Over the centuries, he had taken lovers to test his readiness—to relinquish both Joshu and his own nocturnal existence. More than once he believed he had discovered the perfect mate. In each instance, however, the lover had lost his nerve and had refused to follow Victor into a vampire's life.

And then, after nearly two millennia, a lover had consented. Paul was an artist who'd come to Victor's monastery in Rome to illuminate a manuscript. They had fallen in love, and Victor had turned his new lover into his thrall and then, with Paul's consent, into a vampire. But after the transformation, Victor could not bear to part with Paul. They left the monastery and remained together, in violation of the laws of the Dark Kingdom, until an agent of the kingdom had threatened to take Paul's life.

Now, with his growing power as a vampire maker, Victor believed he could defend those whom he transformed against the forces of the Dark Kingdom. And with every vampire he created, his power would only grow.

His power, he secretly hoped, might serve another purpose. It might enable him, once and for all, to overcome his eternal, unflagging desire for the one lover he could never possess.

When the descending sun left Lafayette's tombs in shadows, Victor opened his eyes in his close resting place, as he had done for two millennia. To claim a tomb as his own gave him a profound delight. He rested like a king in his gilded palace, radiating his power over defenseless subjects even as he lay deceptively still as death. But unlike an earthly king, his own dark power ultimately conquered every living thing.

Now as he pushed open the casket, an intense sense of vulnerability overcame him, as though a powerful enemy had lately lurked in the mausoleum's shadows. He had a vague, dreamlike impression that he had lashed out at an intruder. Was the unsettling feeling simply the remnant of a nightmare? For even beings with his nature could not escape visions that haunted their sleep.

Whatever the source of this feeling, he answered it automatically as he always did, with determination to assert his dominance. The pattern of such a response had begun early in his mortal life in the Roman campagna. He had a clear recollection of a day in his childhood when he had lost a game of chance to his patrician father. They had been sitting among the lush foliage of their villa's courtyard, a servant filling his father's cup with wine. With one roll of the dice, his father had won the game. Sizing Victor up with eyes the color of steel, his father finished his cup and asked, "Now what do you do?"

Victor had immediately showed him. He called for Justin, his favorite brother, who was eventually smothered by their father to spare him from disease. When Justin appeared in the courtyard, Victor had commanded him to pick up one of the wooden swords they used for matches and had lunged at him with his own.

"You are the gladiator, and I am the Roman officer," he'd shouted, squaring off with Justin, whose dark eyes stared admiringly at him. "You have foolishly challenged me to combat. And I have determined to cut you down before the crowd."

"An officer would never engage in such combat," their father interjected, clearly amused.

"But I am the exception," Victor had answered. "I mean to assert the authority of my station. I mean to show even trained gladiators that they are no match for one of my stature and birth."

"So be it," his father said, indulgently waving his hand.

Victor rushed at Justin, again and again knocking the sword from his hand, but allowing him to rearm himself, until in a coup de grace, Victor knocked him to the stone tiles of the courtyard, straddled him, grabbed him by his dark ringlets, and affected to behead him.

"Very well done, my son," his father admitted. "You've accomplished your goal."

"Haven't I though?" he said. The sense of his own strength, and of his birthright to it, coursed through him like the flooded Tiber. And from that moment on, in every moment of jeopardy, this sense of power was his for the summoning.

He summoned it now, and Kyle's innocent face came to his mind as he looked for an object upon which to assert himself. Kyle's little rendezvous with the priest at the cathedral had not, of course, gone unnoticed by Victor. He was attuned to every movement of his thrall, and in his mind's eye—at least during his waking hours—he could see where Kyle was and with whom the young man was keeping company. His thrall's attraction to the priest did not surprise him, considering Kyle's religiosity and the priest's good nature and handsome appearance. And although Victor himself freely indulged his own attractions with handsome strangers, such indulgence must never be pursued by his thrall. Only once Kyle consented to take on a completely nocturnal existence could he pursue any whim that pleased him—though Victor could also destroy anyone he viewed as his competitor, a prerogative that would also belong to Kyle. Yes, compulsions to kneel in the cathedral and take the sacrament were one thing. Compulsions to confide in a priest were another.

It was a short walk from the cemetery to Victor's mansion. When Victor entered it, he stood in the magnificent hall, quiet in its plush upholstery and heavy drapes, and directed his senses to Kyle. He was not in the house, downstairs or up, but his presence was strong. Victor crossed the large room and traveled down the dark, paneled hallway to the glass-encased arboretum at the rear of the house, filled with ficus plants, hydrangeas, ferns, and dark rattan furniture, all visible in the lingering twilight. Victor crossed the arboretum and gazed through the glass. Kyle was on a piece of open lawn framed by thick shrubs and magnolias. In shorts that revealed his muscular thighs, he maneuvered a soccer ball with his feet toward makeshift goalposts he'd erected near the rear wall and sent it sailing through the posts. When he turned around, he caught sight of Victor gazing at him and his own gaze filled with apprehension. Abandoning the ball, he advanced toward the arboretum in obedience to Victor's silent summons.

"You're right," Kyle said when he entered. "You're able to rise earlier and earlier." His face was red from exertion, and his sweaty hair was plastered to his forehead.

"You smell like a dog," Victor said, patting the chest of Kyle's damp T-shirt. "Let's go outside in the fresh air."

They walked out into the yard and sat on an iron bench beneath a magnolia. Victor silently watched Kyle, whose discomfort betrayed him, despite his effort to appear at ease, his elbows on the back of the bench, his bare legs, covered with faint, fair hair, spread out before him.

"Why are you so nervous?" Victor pursued.

"I'm not," Kyle answered without looking at him.

Victor laughed. "You think you can hide your movements from me?"

Kyle turned to him now, alarmed.

"You know I see everything. I don't approve of your friendship with the priest. I'm afraid I'll have to take care of him."

"What do you mean?"

"What do you think I mean?" Victor caressed Kyle's thigh.

"I'll stay away from him."

Victor shook his head. "I don't believe you can. Not the way you are now. Have you given some thought to what I want?"

"Please, Victor. Just leave him alone."

Victor studied him. Kyle's feelings were stronger than he'd suspected. He found this surprisingly irritating. "He doesn't matter. There will always be priests, and you'll always be looking for them."

Kyle opened his mouth to deny it, but saw that it was no use. The horrible consequences of his dalliance with Charles seemed to register in his gray eyes.

"If you agree to the transformation, I'll leave him alone."

"I don't believe you," Kyle said faintly.

Victor chuckled and stood up. "Very good. You're learning." He turned and made his way back to the house.

"Victor!" Kyle shouted after him.

But his call was futile. Victor's course was set.

Like all vampires, Victor could transport himself from one point to the next with the speed of thought when distances were not long. When they were, he could lift into the night's sky and sail to his destination—more like a vulture, he often mused, than the bat figuring in the legends about the undead. But now, he wanted to take his time, to inhale the aroma of blood and human flesh within the residences along St. Charles. He enjoyed the anticipation of taking his unsuspecting prey. He liked imagining the look of horror, the useless attempt to defend, especially when the victim was accustomed to being stronger than anyone around him. This was the case with the priest, a powerful man, whose broad chest and arms would make him a perfect master of the breaststroke, if he were an Olympic swimmer, and whose nature seemed to be the spiritual equivalent of such a master, gathering the grace to himself like water and thrusting it out to the world.

On Bourbon Street, some of the customary liveliness had returned. Residents of the Quarter sat inside the open doors of bars. Zydeco music played in one club and jazz in another. Before long the level of activity on Bourbon would increase to its prehurricane days since the Quarter was intact and an irresistible magnet for tourists. Victor enjoyed leering down at the crowd from a gallery above the street, searching for the perfect throat to satisfy his appetite. Now, he turned on Dumaine and walked two blocks down the dark street to the place he had seen in his mind: the plum-colored building owned by the archdiocese. But when he gazed through the bars of the gate into the courtyard beyond the mews, he knew that the man he sought was not within. The very peculiar aroma of his blood, more metallic than most, was not detectable, and Victor's keen senses could inhale a scent across the distance of a football field. His intuition told him that the priest could be found in the cathedral, and he walked the few blocks to the church's façade on Chartres Street.

A man played a violin there, a basket on the ground for offerings, and near him were the usual tarot card readers, already seated at their tables. As he had done before, Victor moved to the side of the cathedral, out of their sight, and tried the door. There was no need to force it once again; he found it unlocked.

The priest knelt on the sanctuary steps. The only light in church came from the racks of votive candles on either side of the transept and the large vigil candle flickering near the tabernacle, a sign of Christ's presence in the form of consecrated hosts. The priest did not turn his head when Victor entered.

"I figured you'd be coming," he said.

"Very perceptive." Victor approached the priest, hovering over him. "How did you know?"

"Because I know what you are. And I know you want to harm me."

"Are you afraid?"

"Yes, I am. That's why I'm praying."

Victor laughed at the futility of this act, and the bass sound of his voice resonated against the empty church's marble surfaces. "So, what is it you think I am? Surely you don't believe the fantastic story that Kyle told you?" he said. "You can see he's disturbed. Without me, he'd be defenseless."

The priest said nothing. His well-proportioned, hefty body was dressed in a crewneck sweater without a shirt underneath, and his sturdy, thick throat was enticing. But Victor desired to face his victim, to see the fear that the priest would not be able to hide, no matter how pious or stoic or stubborn the man. Victor climbed the sanctuary steps and sprang effortlessly onto the altar, turning to survey his victim and the dark nave beyond.

Now the priest raised his eyes. He was indeed handsome, and his good nature did not abandon him even in this moment of confronting the demonic. Victor had known many a scrupulous, guilt-ridden priest in his many centuries of existence, but rarely had he encountered one with such natural moral strength.

"What if I give you a chance to run?"

"It wouldn't do any good."

"You don't want to try?"

The priest smiled a big grin, as if he were Victor's drinking buddy in the booth of a pub and Victor had just told a joke. "You can't hurt me," he said boldly. "Maybe you can kill me, but you can't hurt my soul."

"No?" The priest's piety rankled him. "What if I make you what he is? So much for your soul's salvation then."

The priest stared at him, in alarm.

The priest's apprehension pleased Victor. He seated himself on the altar and folded his arms, determined to play with this mouse like a cat before the kill.

The priest appeared to rally his courage. "You can never win. Not against God."

Victor scrutinized the priest's eyes, discernible to him even in the darkness of the church. They were as soft and brown as a puppy's. He inhaled the strongly metallic scent of the man's blood. Then suddenly he discerned some kind of force within the priest beyond his own power. Victor jumped down and approached the priest to take a closer look, dropping to one knee and attempting to peer into the man's face, which the priest kept turned from him.

"What do you want from me?" the priest said.

"I want to know why you're lying to me," Victor whispered, bringing his face very close to the priest's. "I want to know what you're hiding."

Now the priest turned his face, ever so slightly, to meet Victor eye to eye. "You can't touch me."

The challenge was too much for Victor to resist. Clasping the priest by the shoulders, he opened his mouth wide, displaying his fangs. He knew that even in the dark, the luminosity of his own lurid complexion made them visible to the priest.

Panicking, the priest tried to free himself. Victor grabbed him by the throat, determined to choke the life out of him. But suddenly Victor found himself unable to exert force. It was as though his will had detached itself from him, unable to communicate with the muscles in his hands. Then a burning sensation shot through his hands and he jerked them away from the priest and stood up.

Now out of his grasp, the priest took the opportunity to get up and flee to the tabernacle at the base of the reredos. He touched the golden doors as though they offered a force of protection. "I know where you are during the day," he shouted. "I know how to free Kyle."

Victor sized up his opponent. Did the priest truly have the nerve it would take to plunge a stick of chiseled wood into a living heart? For a moment Victor felt too stunned to move. Then he saw a strange shadow pass before the priest—the shadow of a woman, hooded it seemed. The presence felt strangely familiar. Not from the present, but rather from the distant past, centuries ago, though still as close to him as recent years are to mortals. It was no ghost of someone he had once known. It was no ghost at all. It was a being with its own formidable power. Perhaps an agent from the Dark Kingdom, come to interfere with his plans.

"Show yourself!" Victor shouted.

But the shadow did not materialize.

"Very well," Victor said, satisfied. He took this reticence as a sign of the creature's intimidation. Despite her power to protect the priest—whatever her reasons—she was apparently no match for him. He turned and walked the whole length of the nave to the front doors of the church, which he snapped open with a single jerk.

In full view of the tarot card readers he vanished into the air.

His mind spun as his body passed through space. Why was this presence protecting the priest? Was she determined to use the priest to draw Kyle away, to keep him from consenting to life as a vampire? If so, there was little time to lose. He must pressure his thrall to accept the partnership he offered him.

When he arrived at the mansion, he entered the front door and lit candles throughout the large front room, on the dark furniture he had purchased from the plantation manor, on the harpsichord, the tables, the shelves. He lit the candles in the two candelabra on the tall mantle, which doubled in number in the enormous mirror behind them, a mirror too high to unsettle anyone by his absent reflection in it. When he had extinguished all of the electric lights, the dark room danced with flames. He put on a recording of Chopin's nocturnes, and closing his eyes and floating on the strains of the piano, he directed his thoughts to Kyle. Within moments the thrall entered the room in a dark velour robe.

"Why look so sad?" Victor said, glaring at Kyle. He'd settled in an armchair, his feet propped on an ottoman.

"Did you . . . hurt him?"

"I don't want to talk about the priest. I want to talk about you and me. Come here."

Kyle approached reluctantly. He started to take a seat on the sofa across from Victor.

"No. Here." Victor moved his feet from the ottoman.

Kyle obeyed. He sat facing Victor.

"If I had hurt him, it would be your fault. Wouldn't it?"

"Yes," Kyle answered meekly.

"Because you took him to my resting place. So, you put him in jeopardy—with your own hands."

"I didn't look at it that way. There wouldn't have been any need. I mean, he would never have tried to hurt you."

"How could you be so sure?" Victor scrutinized Kyle's pale face. The young man did seem confident that the priest would not have tried anything in the crypt. If he had done so, as they both knew, Kyle's instinctive response would have been to end the priest's life. The thrall's nature commanded it. When it came to protecting his vampire host, a thrall had no choice but to move swiftly and severely. A thrall could never allow the one upon whom he depended for his own existence to undergo harm. This was true despite Kyle's suicidal impulses caused by the turmoil in his soul. Kyle might destroy himself, but he could never threaten Victor's life, and if anyone else tried to do so, Kyle—with a face so guileless and a temperament so pious—would have crushed the offender.

"You know what I want from you?" Victor leaned forward and stroked Kyle's knee. "I want a lover like Paul. My equal. Someone with strength to be himself, even to stand up to me."

"It never did him any good."

"You don't know that!" Victor snapped. "I loved him. I left him in order to save his life. It was the first sacrifice of my long life." The shy hazel eyes of the artist he had loved came to his mind. Four years had passed since they had parted. Paul believed that Victor had taken his rightful place in the Dark Kingdom, that in two hundred years they would be reunited. The lie was a necessary one. If Paul had known that Victor had fled to another earthly region, Paul would have pursued him. And to Victor's objection that Paul's life was at stake—that the Dark Kingdom would destroy Paul, if necessary, to prevent association that violated the order of their existence—Paul would have shrugged, willing to risk annihilation rather than eternal separation.

Of course, one way to have appeased Paul, as well as the powers of the Dark Kingdom, would have been to obey the laws governing a vampire's existence. But that sacrifice was too much for Victor. Now that he'd stubbornly determined to keep his absolute, albeit solitary, power on earth, obedience to the laws meant crawling like a snake on its belly.

"And what if you had to abandon me, the way you abandoned him? At least this way, the way we are—" Kyle could not finish the admission he clearly recognized that he was making.

Victor stood and pulled him to his feet. He kissed the young man passionately, forcing his tongue through Kyle's lips, grinding his erect penis into Kyle's crotch. Kyle yielded to him, wrapping his arms around him and sucking Victor's tongue as though his life depended on it.

Victor finally pulled his mouth away and whispered into Kyle's ear, "See how much you want me."

"Yes," Kyle muttered, trying to catch his breath. "Like a thrall."

Smiling, Victor shook his head. "That's not true. It's not because you're forced to. You love me of your own free will."

"Then I'm an idiot," Kyle said.

"You think I couldn't love you. I don't blame you. I've never been the sentimental type. Not in my life before this existence. Not now. I've practiced cold detachment for two millennia, cutting my losses whenever necessary. But I'm telling you now that I do love you. Listen to me. Don't you want to be freed from this slavery to religious piety? Don't you want to breathe like a free being for once in your life? Admit it. You love me."

"Yes," Kyle whispered, his eyes filling.

"You know you shouldn't. But you do. Love is mysterious that way."

"I suppose you ought to know."

"Yes, I should. I've lived long enough. Here." Victor ripped his fangs into his wrist and pressed it to Kyle's mouth.

Kyle grabbed Victor hungrily, his nostrils distended, his eyelids fluttering in lusty delirium as he began to drink. Then Victor yanked his wrist away. Bloody-mouthed, Kyle screwed up his face like a baby whose bottle has been withdrawn.

"What are you doing?" he blurted.

"I have something better for you." Victor tore open his shirt and offered his breast to Kyle. "Join me in a new life," he said, guiding Kyle's mouth to his nipple. "A vampire's life."

Taken off guard, hungry for blood, Kyle hesitated only an instant before mouthing Victor's nipple. But as he began to suck, someone suddenly pounded on the front door, and Kyle pulled his head away. "Who's that?" he said in a voice slurred by his appetites.

Victor gazed toward the sound. He knew who it was. He sensed the presence of the priest. Charles must have followed him from the cathedral. He must have climbed over the mansion's iron gate.

As the pounding grew more desperate, Kyle recovered himself, backing away from Victor. Then the priest appeared at one of the tall windows, peering in through a gap in the drapes. When he discerned Kyle in the candlelight, he began pounding frantically on the glass.

"Charles!" Kyle looked longingly at the window.

Furious that the spell had been broken, Victor grabbed Kyle, and for benefit of the visitor, who could no doubt see them clearly, tore off Kyle's robe. He bent him over the back of the sofa, opened his own trousers and, excited at the sight of Kyle's smooth, white buttocks, thrust himself into Kyle's anus. Kyle shouted in pain, but as Victor hammered away, the thrall began moaning in pleasure.

The priest continued to pound the window, clearly frantic to rescue Kyle from the assault. But when Kyle reached for Victor's wrist, kissed it, and greedily resumed drinking from it, the pounding ceased. Gloating, and at the point of climax, Victor saw the priest's face fall. As he exploded in orgasm, he threw back his head. When he had spent himself, he lowered his gaze, directing it back to the window. Charles had disappeared.

6

I can see you are troubled, Charles. I think we should forgo the plethysmograph procedure today and discuss the matters on your mind." Seated with her legs crossed, Dr. Beauchamp stared intently at Charles. She wore an indigo shift, and her hair was tied back with a scarf with a leopard-skin design. She was stunning in the soft lamplight of the room, her dreadlocks gathered at the top of her head and showering down like a dark cataract.

"Is it that obvious?" Charles said. He was seated across from Dr. Beauchamp. He was exhausted and restless. He hadn't had a good night's sleep for days.

"Yes. I could see it in your eyes the moment I opened the door. What is it?"

Charles hesitated. He had replayed everything in his mind, again and again: the blazing altar and the apparition of Kyle; Charles's loss of consciousness at Victor's mansion only to wake, inexplicably, in his own bed; Kyle's confession; the scene inside the mausoleum at Lafayette Cemetery. Charles had imagined putting it all into words for Beauchamp, but each time he did he knew how it would sound. Like a psychotic fantasy. But now, facing her, he longed to get it off his chest, no matter how she received it all. "You won't believe it," he finally said. "But here goes."

He told her everything, and if she thought he was a lunatic, her dark eyes never betrayed her assessment. They remained fixed intently on him, devoid of emotion.

"I can't believe the words coming out of my mouth," he concluded, "so I guess I don't expect you to, either. But I saw what I saw."

"I don't think you're insane," Beauchamp said in her sonorous voice. "I don't know what to think. You obviously don't believe this all happened with smoke and mirrors. You've thought of that, I'm sure."

"The man had no pulse. And then in a split second, he almost choked me to death. No, it was real—all too real, in fact. I mean, it should feel like a nightmare. Shouldn't it? Like something I couldn't possibly believe. Or like a horror movie. But it feels real—it is real. It did happen. And I knew that Victor would come for me afterwards."

"Come for you?"

Charles told her about Victor's attack in the cathedral. "God must have been protecting me."

Beauchamp nodded solemnly in agreement. "He protects his own." She studied Charles for a moment. "But there's something more. Tell me."

Charles looked away. The irony of his discomfort struck him. Without flinching, he had just recounted his encounter with a vampire. But when he thought of confessing the desperation he had felt as he pounded on the window of Victor's mansion—as he saw Kyle give himself to Victor and drink from the man's wrist—he found his tongue tied. The pain of it was too deep, too personal. He was afraid of what it meant. "I can't talk about it," he finally said.

Beauchamp reflected for a moment. "I see. I'd like to pray with you, Charles."

Beauchamp lit the candle that sat on the glass-top table in front of her.

"Now, close your eyes," she said.

Charles obeyed.

"O God of light and darkness, you see the mysteries of the universe, while we grope blindly. You know that evil takes many shapes and threatens always to overwhelm us with its dark power. Reveal the truth to this son, who has encountered such evil." Beauchamp prayed with such authority that she seemed almost to command God rather than plead with him. "Give him the strength and wisdom to resist its power and to save the one who has succumbed to it. You have consecrated your son. You have also consecrated the one seduced by the force of evil. May the consecration that they both share be the means of their salvation. You never abandon your own. You supply them with a shield and buckler to defeat Lucifer and all his minions. Be with your son as he enters the fray to save your own. In the name of the Father, the Son, and the Holy Ghost."

Charles opened his eyes and found that tears streamed down Beauchamp's cheeks. Her eyes were fixed with determination on him.

"Then you do believe me," he said.

"The supernatural realm is real. Whether we can ever understand it or not is another question. But I don't waste my time on speculation. This young man needs your help, Charles. You must save him."

"How?" Charles said, desperate. "I can't force him to leave Victor. And even if I could, he'd just go back to him. He's in Victor's power."

"Don't be so sure. He's a priest. That gives him strength. With your help, he can break away."

"But what if Victor retaliates? What if he tries to hurt Kyle?"

"Have faith. You've already experienced one miracle. This will be another. In fact, your cure may have been a preparation for this mission."

Charles could hold back his fears no longer. "What if I'm not cured? What I feel for Kyle . . . what if it's not just his soul I care about?" He felt the blood rushing to his face.

Beauchamp remained unmoved. "All the more reason to help him. You can prove to yourself that you can resist your attractions. Isn't that what we're working on in our sessions? You expose yourself to the images on that screen." She nodded to the computer behind him. "You face your temptations rather than fleeing from them. Fleeing never works. The more one runs, the more one is pursued. I've treated anxiety in the same way. I asked my clients who suffer from anxiety attacks to provoke the feelings they dread. To sit with them and stare them in the face. This is the way to discover that you are a master of your own fate and not at the mercy of external forces."

"But anxiety is inside a person, not an external force."

"True, in some respects. But anxiety has its source in real experiences. Abuse, rejection, failure. Besides, we're speaking about attraction. It's one's own weak flesh that tempts one. Show yourself that you can overcome it. A priest must serve everyone—despite his own attractions or prejudices. All are equal for the one called to guide his sheep."

The words relieved Charles. Beauchamp had to be right. He couldn't abandon Kyle. This attraction—it was just a test. And he would pass it.

When he left her office that evening, his restlessness was gone. A ton of bricks seemed to have been removed from his shoulders. He went home, crawled into bed, and slept soundly for the first time in a week.

The next evening he got a call from a parishioner whose son was dying of cancer. The family had returned to New Orleans despite the man's illness because he wanted to die at home. The family would have preferred the monsignor to come because they knew him well, but the monsignor was visiting his own relatives in Chicago. So Charles stuffed his stole and prayer book into a backpack and rode to the Garden District. The vine-covered Italianate mansion was only two blocks from Victor and Kyle's home, and he felt uneasy standing on another porch so close to theirs. The night was cool and humid. Drizzle fell on the heavy foliage of the neighborhood.

Mrs. Jadoun, a gentle, plump old woman barely five feet tall, welcomed him at the door and led him through an elegantly furnished bedroom on the first floor. A swarthy man lay unconscious under the sheets. He looked to be in his early forties, hints of gray in his goatee. His weary father, white-headed and proper-looking in a sweater vest and tie, sat in a chair by the bed, holding his son's hand. And a middle-aged woman with a stethoscope around her neck stood on the other side of the bed, stroking the young man's head. A scented candle burned in the stuffy room, the walls lined with books, but the smells of disinfectant and sickness were too strong to hide.

Charles put on his stole and read the prayers for the dying while he anointed the man's forehead with oil. Then everyone knelt around the bed, and he led the sorrowful mysteries of the rosary. With odd regularity the father sobbed each time he announced a mystery: the agony in the garden, the carrying of the cross, the crucifixion . . . After reciting the rosary a strange thing happened. As Charles stood near the bed, a vision of Victor in his coffin superimposed itself on the dying man. Victor's handsome features, dark hair, and powerful body were as clear and real as they were the day Charles had beheld them in the eerie tomb. Involuntarily Charles jumped back, trying to calm himself for the family's sake, but when the man's eyes suddenly snapped open, he started.

"You'll die!" Victor said, stretching his mouth to reveal long canines, so sharp they might have been filed.

"Jesus!" Charles blurted, his heart pounding.

"What's wrong, Father?" Mrs. Jadoun said in alarm.

Charles tried to calm himself. He told himself that he couldn't be seeing Victor. This strange vision was not real. But his panic did not subside until he glanced up at the crucifix near the wall by the door. Then when his eyes returned to the bed, Victor was no more.

He stayed until two in the morning, when the man took his last breath. The exhausted old couple seemed relieved. Bleary-eyed, they thanked him for coming and said they would call him about the funeral arrangements.

When Charles stepped into the night air, the dampness made him shiver. He glanced up and down the quiet street apprehensively, with an eerie sense that Victor was close by, and sped away on his Vespa.

He fell asleep immediately upon climbing into bed and dreamed of Victor. In a lavender silk shirt, Victor stood over his bed, baring his teeth, blood streaming from the corners of his mouth. Charles shouted out in his sleep and the sound of his own voice woke him. For a moment, he thought someone was standing over him. He sprang to his feet, only to find the room empty. All the same, he switched on a lamp, grabbed his rosary from the bed table, and placed it around his neck, finally falling back to sleep under the lamplight.

The next morning, Charles returned to the Garden District and watched outside the gate of Victor's mansion, looking for a sign that Kyle stirred within it. As he had done before, he finally used the Vespa as a step ladder and crawled over the iron gate. The drapes were completely drawn behind the long windows, so he didn't bother trying to peer into the house. Instead he walked around the house, inspecting the windows under the magnolia branches. But all were darkened by drapery.

In the back of the house, however, two windows on the second floor were uncovered. He called out Kyle's name. For a second, he thought he saw someone at the window.

"Kyle," he shouted again. "Let me in."

But Kyle's face did not appear and the only response was silence.

Finally, he turned away. He climbed the fence with the help of a bench from the backyard, then boarded his Vespa, and rode off toward the Quarter.

The next morning, after another uneasy night, Charles's mother called. He stood in his terry cloth bathrobe on the gallery, cell phone in hand. The sky above was hazy, and dampness lingered after a predawn storm.

His mother's tone concerned him. Like him, she wasn't one to lose sleep over problems, but this morning she sounded worried.

"What's wrong?" Charles said.

"It's Pete. He's acting strange." She spoke with the classic New Orleans accent, a Brooklyn brogue tempered by Southern strains. "Yesterday, he didn't go to class. You know he never misses. God forbid. Remember in high school, I couldn't talk him into staying at home when he had the flu? Threw up all over the boy in front of him."

Charles's brother Pete was a quintessential introverted geek. But he was a nice-looking, sweet kid, and people took to him. In the high school episode, the boy he'd soiled had actually given him a ride home. Pete was now a freshman at the University of New Orleans, which had only recently resumed classes. For the first months of the semester, he'd been accepted by Ole Miss in Oxford, Mississippi.

"Is he sick?" Charles asked, picking up his mug of coffee from the little table on the balcony.

"He says he feels fine. He doesn't have a fever. He's just in a daze. Stares out his window. He hasn't even turned on his computer, and you know how much time he spends on that. He won't say two words. Your father tried talking to him. I tried talking to him. He didn't want dinner last night. I don't know, maybe he's depressed. But he's never been depressed. You think this could be that post-traumatic stuff that Oprah was talking about on her show? After Katrina and all?"

"Heck if I know," Charles said. "I'll come over and talk to him."

"Good. I'm on my way to the hotel, so I'll see you later."

Charles's mother was a housekeeper at a quaint guesthouse in the Quarter, where help was scarce since many hotel workers were from neighborhoods still evacuated.

Charles decided to walk to his family house in Faubourg Marigny, the neighborhood on the other side of Esplanade, which formed the western boundary of the Quarter. He showered and shaved and donned jeans and a sweatshirt. It was Thursday, his day off, and there was no need for clerical attire.

Restaurant and shop employees along Dumaine were hosing

down the sidewalks in front of their businesses. Locals and tourists streamed in and out of the coffee bar on the corner. Charles turned down Royal Street, lined with small hotels and antique shops, and crossed Esplanade into the Marigny. The neighborhood was once completely working-class, full of modest shotgun houses, but like the Quarter, gentrification had invaded. Many houses had been transformed into bed and breakfasts or restaurants. Elegant remodeling had turned others into top-dollar dwellings, amid lush, tropical foliage. Charles passed the bright shutters of many renovated homes on his way to his parents' dingy clapboard structure. The wooden porch sloped, and two of the shutters had become detached at the bottom. His father was a great plumber but not much of a carpenter. Still, the home had its charm. Baskets of violet and pink geraniums hung from the porch ceiling. The bracketed eaves reached out like the wings of a mother hen.

He used his key to open the front door and stepped in. A long hallway inside ran along the rooms of the house: two bedrooms, a bathroom, a long living room, and a kitchen. The smell of coffee lingered from breakfast. Family photos covered the hallway wall.

"Pete," Charles called, rapping on the first door and opening it without awaiting a response.

His brother sat at the window in the rolling chair from his desk, where his computer rested, the monitor blank. His dark, curly hair was uncombed. He wore a gray T-shirt and corduroy trousers. His nicely shaped feet, exact reproductions of Charles's feet, were bare. He didn't turn to look at Charles when he entered.

"Hey. What's up?"

Pete shook his head in response, still staring out the window. Charles approached him and clapped his hands on his brother's broad shoulders. "You okay? Pete!" Charles wheeled the chair around and sat on Pete's unmade bed, against a wall plastered with astronomy charts.

Now Pete looked at him. His brown eyes lacked their usual spark. "I'm fine," he said, quietly.

"Yeah? You don't seem so fine. Why aren't you in class?"

Pete shrugged. "I'm not up to it, today."

Puzzled, Charles stared at him. There was a large Band-Aid on his throat. "What happened?" Charles asked, pointing to Pete's throat.

"I think I cut it shaving."

"You think?"

"Well, I must have."

Heavy stubble covered Pete's long throat. Like Charles, he'd started shaving when he was fifteen. "Then it must have been a while ago."

Pete hesitated and then sighed, as though he'd resolved something. He reached up and stripped off the Band-Aid. Two small, round wounds appeared, about two inches apart. They were still red, as though the injury had happened recently.

"God!" Charles got up and inspected the holes. The flesh was pierced by two sharp points the size of nails. "When did this happen?"

"I woke up with them the day before yesterday. Then again today."

"What do you mean? There are only two marks."

"Two nights ago, I dreamed that someone stood over my bed, and when I woke up, I swore someone was standing there. But then I guess I went back to sleep, and you know how it is—when you finally wake up you're sure that it was all a dream, even the part that seemed real. Except my neck hurt, and I felt weak. And ashamed, as though . . . I don't know." Pete dropped his gaze. His dark lashes seemed thicker than ever now.

"Come on," Charles urged. "You can tell me."

Pete glanced up for a moment but couldn't bear to look at Charles. "I felt like someone raped me."

"You were hurt somewhere else?" Alarmed, Charles touched his brother's shoulder.

"No. I mean, I don't think so. It's just this feeling."

Charles felt relieved. "You said it happened again."

Pete nodded. "I had the same dream last night. I woke up with a man standing over me, then fell back asleep. When I woke up this morning . . . everything felt the same. You think I'm losing it, Charles? Could these be insect bites or something? Because it sounds like something out of a Dracula movie."

Charles sat back down on the bed, trying to absorb the truth. It was clear to him. Victor had done this. Why? Simply to warn Charles to leave Kyle alone—if he wanted Pete unharmed? Or to retaliate against him? If so, how far did Victor intend to go in seeking satisfaction? Would he threaten Pete's life? Panic welled up inside of Charles, but he made himself calm down, for his brother's sake. There was no reason to scare him to death. "I don't know what could have done it," he lied, to assuage Pete's fears. "Maybe some kind of spider."

"Then what about the dream, and the feeling?"

"It was just a creepy nightmare."

Pete shook his head. "I don't know."

"Well, it sure as hell wasn't a ghoul, was it?" Charles joked—convincingly, he hoped. "Look, you've been under a lot of stress. You just start college, then have to evacuate the city and go someplace strange. Then you come back to a disaster area. They're still finding bodies in the Ninth Ward. All the TV coverage. That takes a toll on you. On all of us."

"I guess." Pete did not sound persuaded.

"The best thing you can do is head to class. I mean it. Get your stuff together and take off for the university. Really. Right now. You need to get out of this room. Get your mind off this. Tell you what. You get yourself ready. I'll make you one of my famous omelettes. Is there some ham in the fridge?"

Pete managed a smiled. "Yeah."

Charles went to the kitchen and began assembling the ingredients he needed. As he cooked, he tried to stay calm. He knew what he had to do. He had no choice. He didn't have the slightest doubt that Victor was responsible for the wounds, and who knew how far Victor would go? *The man's really dead anyway,* he told himself. *You wouldn't really be killing someone.* He could think of the body—without a pulse, without respiration—as the carcass of an animal that he had to stab just once. That's all there was to it.

Pete seemed in a better mood as he sat at the counter eating his omelette. He'd cleaned up and shaved. A fresh Band-Aid covered the wounds. When he'd finished his breakfast, he grabbed his backpack, loaded with books, and left the house through the front door. From the window, Charles watched him climb into his fifteen-year-old Honda Civic, the gray paint on the trunk dull with age. When he drove safely away, Charles went out to the shed behind the house. The old campaign sign he remembered was still there. Red lettering said, "Vote for Carl Lamette, City Council." He tore off the cardboard sign, then found a saw and trimmed the stake to one foot. He grabbed a hammer and returned with it and the stake to the kitchen, where he found a nutpick in a drawer full of odds and ends. He deposited the tools in an old backpack from Pete's closet. He looked at Pete's bed, imagining Victor's form hovering over it. *This has to happen*, he told himself.

Riding through the Quarter to St. Charles, he tried to keep focused on the road, imagining that he was going on a routine errand. But his mouth was dry with apprehension. And questions popped up in his mind. What if the stake business was just a bunch of crap from horror movies? What if it only enraged Victor and he attacked again? What if Victor attacked before he had the chance to raise the stake over his heart? And what if the whole vampire thing was just a grotesque trick after all?

No. He'd seen what he'd seen. Not only was he saving Pete, but he was saving Kyle, and anyone else Victor decided to torment.

When he reached Lafayette Cemetery, he secured his bike to a telephone pole outside the walls. It was only eleven, so the gate was still open, although no one was in sight. His heart thudded as he entered, the equipment he needed on his back. He walked through the cemetery and found two tourists strolling down one of the narrow lanes, gray-haired women in sneakers and hooded sweatshirts. He greeted them and continued walking as they stopped to inspect the dates on a mausoleum so old that the engraving was hardly discernible. He waited around the corner, hoping they would soon exit Lafayette. He wanted no one in the cemetery when he entered Victor's tomb. But when he considered the chances that even more people might enter as he waited, unrealistically, to have the whole place to himself, he gave up waiting and made for Victor's tomb.

His hands were sweating as he studied the lock, glancing from side to side to make sure the lane was empty. The lock was original, probably opened with a skeleton key. Who would worry about the easy access? How much security did dusty mausoleums require? He removed his backpack and dug out the nutpick. Crouching, he inserted it into the lock and maneuvered it to find the spring. It didn't take long before he felt the right click. He stood and took a deep breath. *O my God, I am heartily sorry for having offended thee.* The Act of Contrition came automatically to his mind. If this was the last action he took, he wanted to die repentant. *Help me out, here, God!* he added. *If it's wrong, stop me. If it's right, give me strength!*

He replaced the pick in the backpack and pulled out the stake and hammer before slipping it on again. In its proper place the backpack would be out of his way. Checking the lane one last time, he nudged the door open. The gray light revealed the coffin he'd seen before. It was sealed and quietly waiting for him. He hesitated. He'd brought no flashlight! And if he closed the door, he would be forced to fumble in the dark to open the coffin and then find the ghastly, luminous face of Victor. It occurred to him that if he left the door open the daylight, however meager, might disable or even destroy Victor. According to vampire lore, the undead could not survive the light of the sun. Yet, Kyle had told him that as long as Victor remained in his coffin he was safe, so if Kyle was right, the daylight would not relieve Charles of the task ahead. Still, perhaps the light would at least rob Victor of the strength he had exercised the last time Charles had entered this tomb. He also reminded himself of the strange power he had to ward off Victor in the cathedral—power granted him, no doubt, by God. And although to leave the door ajar might increase the risk of being discovered by the two women or other visitors, the idea of it brought Charles more assurance than fear. So with the stone floor of the tomb washed in gray daylight, he proceeded to the coffin.

He crossed himself and touched the cold lid, searching for the latch, which he found. His heart beat so frantically that he had the irrational thought that Victor might hear it and awaken. He drew in a breath. In one quick movement he opened the coffin.

Victor slept there peacefully. This steadied Charles. Rather than being frightened by his luminescence, Charles found Victor beautiful, like a marble statue of a god in repose—strong, youthful, magnificent. The fierceness of his gaze in his waking hours had vanished. Beholding him in this state, Charles could understand why Victor had such power to seduce. Charles hesitated. Then, for his own peace of mind, he placed his hand under Victor's nose. He felt no breath. Reluctantly, cautiously, he reached for Victor's wrist. He kept his fingers on the icy flesh until he was sure there was no pulse.

Then he felt for Victor's sternum through his gray silk shirt, positioned the stake above it to the left, between his ribs. A panicky thought occurred to him. *Where exactly is the heart? What if I miss?* In the movies, the vampire destroyers always proceeded as though the fatal impalement was inevitable. But wasn't it possible to miss the target? If so, was it possible to try another shot, before the vampire attacked?

Sweat trickled down his sides now beneath his sweatshirt. He had to stop thinking and simply act. He raised the hammer over the stake and gritted his teeth. But before he could bring it down, someone blocked the light coming through the door.

"No!" Kyle shouted, lunging at Charles and tackling him.

On the floor, Charles tried to push Kyle off his body, but his strength was too much for him.

"You'll send him to hell," Kyle said.

"It's where he belongs."

"And you'll kill me. I can't survive without him." Kyle's anguished pale face was visible in the dark.

"The hell you can't!"

"I mean it. I need to feed on him. If you kill him, you kill me. I shouldn't care. I've wanted God to take me. But I can't do it like this."

Charles felt confused. Should he believe Kyle? Or was Kyle so much under Victor's power that he would say anything to protect him?

"I'll go away with you," Kyle suddenly blurted.

"How can you? If you need him?"

Kyle got up and stood over Victor. He raised Victor's arm. Unbuttoning the silk sleeve, he tore at the inside of Victor's forearm with his teeth. Victor's arm twitched, but he did not rise up from the coffin. Charles moved away, recoiling from what he saw: Kyle lapped at Victor's flesh the way he had as Charles gazed at them through their window.

Kyle's gray eyes, fixed on Charles as he drank, were as wild and frightening as those of a wolf.

PART II

PURGATORIO

e canterò di quel secondo regno
dove l'umano spirito si purga
e di salire al ciel diventa degno.

*(And I will sing of that second kingdom
where the human spirit is purged
and becomes fit to ascend to Heaven.)*

—Dante Alighieri

7

In his sleep, Victor was aware of nothing in the present moment, not the musty odor of the mausoleum, not his own cool flesh or shallow, infrequent breaths. His mind had moved far back in time, two thousand years back. On horseback, he had arrived at a stone synagogue in Nazareth. Before he could dismount, a mob poured through the doors, and someone moved among the throng like a conch in the tide. Victor caught sight of the victim. It was Joshu. From his mount, Victor ordered the crowd to desist, but his voice was drowned by the shouting. The synagogue rose on a hillside, not far from a cliff, and the crowd moved toward the rocky precipice. Victor charged forward, nearly trampling several people. Just in time, however, they drew aside. Then, as the rioters registered that he was a Roman officer, they scattered in fear.

But Joshu was nowhere to be seen. For a moment Victor believed that the mob had pushed him over the precipice. He approached it, dismounted, and peered down to the ravine below. There was no sign of a body.

"Who are you looking for?" Joshu's voice was full of amusement.

Victor turned to find Joshu, unscathed and smiling, dressed in a homespun tunic.

"What roused them?"

Joshu shrugged. "I only said that I've come to proclaim good news to the poor. And to outsiders—because my own people weren't worthy of God."

"So you offended the wealthy merchants. And everyone else! And in your hometown. Not wise to bite the hand that feeds you."

"Man does not live by bread alone, Victor," Joshu teased, slapping Victor's shoulder. Joshu's face was browned by the sun. His dark, captivating eyes sparkled.

Victor grabbed his hand. He longed to be done with this never-ending play, either to leave Joshu or to kill him. He could not force Joshu to submit. With Joshu, everything was different.

"I've begun now," Joshu said. "What I've talked about for the past year. My mission. It's time to usher in the Final Age, when the sky turns to blood and the moon plummets to the earth. As you can see, this is not what people want to hear."

"Then it's foolish to proclaim it. Why should anyone want to listen?"

"Because whoever awakens will truly live, not just survive. Whoever awakens will discover passion, and courage, and hope, and joy."

"Because of a fantasy world? You may preach that man does not live by bread alone, but reality will rear its head once you deprive your followers of it."

Joshu laughed. He snatched up a stone from the ground and flung it over the precipice. "I won't deprive anyone. Whoever walks in my steps will find nourishment, for my yoke is easy, my burden light."

"Why can't you see the fulfillment I offer you?" Victor said.

Joshu stared intently at him. "Tell me this. Why do you care? Are you really concerned about my fulfillment or your own lust?"

"Don't play the sophist with me. I've had enough of Greek philosophers."

"I love you, Victor."

"I'm not interested in words."

"Follow me."

Victor gazed back at him in wonder. "You're serious!"

"Yes, the gall of it. I'm a Judean subject. An artisan's son. But you can't leave me alone. Why? What is this power I have over you?"

"I wish to God I knew."

"I know. Come with me, and you'll know, too."

There was no reasoning with such a demented man. The incomprehensibility of Joshu's words left Victor speechless. This time, when he turned to go, he vowed to himself he would never seek Joshu again.

But he did, again and again.

And he heard reports in Jerusalem of a Galilean who healed the sick and even raised the dead. He believed it. He knew Joshu's powers of persuasion and of conjuring.

He was not one to probe into human motivation, but he did ponder Joshu's. Why live among the rabble, lepers and beggars and children and women? Why, when one had the charisma and face and physique of Joshu? If he wanted to provoke the authorities of Rome, why not raise an army, as Joshu might do without difficulty? There were enough young malcontents among the Judeans.

The rest of his history with Joshu advanced through Victor's sleeping mind. Not like a dream, but like an account shaped into a movie, with camera close-ups and fading shots. Modern forms of media had left their mark on Victor's ancient mind, a mind with nearly digital sharpness and retention. Victor's mind appropriated into its eternal mechanism the new technology of every age. Even in sleep, Victor sensed that his mind had organized the account for some purpose. His unconscious mind attuned itself to whatever cosmic message the scenes might hold. The drama ended with a flash of light, perhaps the flash that punctuated Joshu's last earthly parting from him the morning of Joshu's resurrection from the dead.

Victor's eyes opened. He rose and hurried to feel the lingering rays of the sun, a sensation that would have tortured his skin, might even have destroyed him, before his newfound strength had come to him. On the way to his mansion, a girl whizzed by him on a skateboard. He was hungry, and he considered following her to feed, but he thought better of it. Better to save his appetite for the priest's brother.

As he started for the Marigny to feed on the boy, he suddenly remembered his dream with astounding vividness. Then a sense of Joshu's presence overcame him. It was as though he and Joshu were still in their mortal existence—as though they had just parted hours ago and now Joshu was calling him back. But the invitation came from a strange direction, not from the cathedral or the quiet, empty alleys of the Quarter. The summons came from a more remote, grisly part of the city: the lower Ninth Ward, which bore the brunt of the hurricane's flooding. Victor lifted into the air and soared to the place of ruin. He lighted on an abandoned car. All around, boxlike homes stood empty, many of their doors marked with a sign indicating to recovery teams that a body lay within.

Mud replaced yards. Overturned cars collected in one yard,

probably on lower ground than surrounding yards and tossed there by the flood. Some windows in the forlorn houses had been boarded, but in most houses, vacant, glassless holes stared out at the mud-filled street. The scent of decomposing bodies reeked in Victor's supersensitive nostrils. This kind of raw, sweet decay, unmingled with the earth, was offensive to Victor. There was no comfort in it, as there was in the fragrance of the cemetery, where the odor of decay was more akin to a ripening cheese or aging wine than this putrid, garbage-sweet scent.

Victor had no idea why Joshu had summoned him here, but whatever the reason, it didn't matter. He would have rushed to meet Joshu on even the most forlorn place on earth.

Not a single streetlight glowed. Not a single sign of life lingered in the abandoned neighborhood. Victor trudged up the street, past an abandoned gas station. He closed his eyes and let himself be led to a clearing that once must have been a park. Large oaks grew there, the leaves on their highest branches still intact.

He discerned the silhouette of someone sitting on a bench ahead and approached it. The broad, sloping shoulders, the handsome profile belonged unmistakably to Joshu. When he stood directly in front of him, Joshu looked up at him. Light from the full moon rising over eastern housetops fell on his face, the face of a vibrant young man of thirty, with a well-shaped brow, high cheekbones, and determined yet gentle eyes. If it were possible to combine the attitude of a confident CEO and a nurturing lover, the result would be the expression on Joshu's face. He was wearing a long tunic, with sleeves that crawled up on his sinewy arms as he raised them to the back of the bench.

"Where have you been?" he said.

"Where have *you* been?" Victor answered. His heart raced.

"Never far away."

"No, just an ice age away in that sterile heaven of yours."

"That's what I want to talk to you about."

"Heaven?" Victor laughed. He took a seat next to Joshu, Joshu's arm extending cozily behind him. "Why would your heaven interest me?"

"I'm there."

"Not the way I want you. I don't intend to join a throng of worshipers around your throne. Statues. They only wound up there because of their ignorance. If they'd known what lay ahead . . . But I suppose even if they did, they would choose it—considering the alternative in your eternal sphere. The fires of hell, lapping their souls forever. Absurd alternatives."

Joshu smiled. "You want to believe that's the way it is. So you can continue living in this nightmare of yours. A world of darkness, of preying on the weak."

"I'm emperor of this dark world. And if I chose, I could leave it for my own heaven."

"But you don't choose to go there. Why not?"

Victor studied Joshu's calm face for a sign of self-righteousness, of mockery. He found none. Joshu, as always, waited for the real answer.

"I've been master of my own existence for two thousand years. Can you say that? Your earthly submission to your God has continued through eternity."

"You see it that way because of how you understand power. For you power is forcing someone to fear you. You think death is the ultimate reality, and so do the people you terrorize. But death is not the ultimate reality."

"I have no interest in metaphysics, Joshu. I only understand flesh and blood things. Especially blood." Victor laughed. He tried to slap Joshu's thigh, but his hand encountered nothing but air. Joshu's ethereal, inaccessible nature angered him. "Yes, you've long ago abandoned flesh and blood. You're an illusion. Maybe my mind is creating you."

"You know better than that. I'm real. And I love you."

"Me and millions."

"You can't deplete love. It's the true power."

"So your eternity is a love feast?"

"It's a mystery that only love can teach you. When you know true love, you'll know heaven. It's not about submitting. It's about an end to all isolation, being connected to everything and everyone, including your deepest self. Right now, you know only solitude and the brute force that preserves it. Your view of the universe is distorted. Except . . ."

"Except what?"

"Except that your desires are pointing you to the truth at every moment."

"What desires?"

"Your desire for union—with someone, with me. Listen to it." Joshu stood and turned around to survey the devastation around him. His tunic fluttered in the breeze. "See this desolated place? It's what brute force like yours creates."

"Don't blame this on me. Where was your God when the hurricane struck?"

"In pain. And still in pain for all these people. That's what you don't understand."

"You're right."

Joshu turned without offering to further enlighten him and walked toward a dilapidated house with a hole punched in the roof. The occupants must have broken through it as the waters rose around them. They must have been among those who waited to be rescued amid the putrid flood around them. The door of the house was marked with paint. Did the sign indicate that all occupants had been rescued? Or did it indicate that bodies remained within? From the pungent scent that suddenly reached him through the wind, Victor knew the answer. Joshu stood in the muddy yard and waited. The door opened, and a dark figure emerged, hesitating, then joyfully running to Joshu's arms. In an instant, both faded from sight.

Victor involuntarily started toward the house, as if to follow Joshu and the soul he had embraced. It was not that he seriously considered Joshu's invitation. No part of his vampire consciousness and no part of his abiding Roman consciousness—the consciousness of a privileged member of the Empire—responded to an invitation that struck his ears like a foreign language or, more dramatically, like the fanatical, self-destructive language of a primitive native of some earlier time who longed to offer himself as a sacrifice to a tribal god. It was another, more buried place in his consciousness that longed to pursue Joshu. It had nothing to do with a submission incomprehensible to him, but rather with a mysterious expansion of spirit promised to him and related somehow to the love Joshu had expressed for him in his earthly life, a love not universal and noble but particular and unmistakeably erotic.

Frustrated by his longing, Victor instinctively desired to assert his power, and not by merely toying with the priest's brother. He would confront the priest himself and secure his thrall.

He soared away from the dark, devastated neighborhood, lighting in the Quarter. To gain strength, he fed on a man seated on the front stoop of his clapboard shotgun, throwing him to the sidewalk before the man could even try to defend himself. Victor drank only what he needed, leaving the man to recover. Newly energized, he set out for Dumaine.

No lights glowed in the building facing the street. But through the iron gate he saw lights in the windows of the priest's apartment at the rear of the courtyard. There was no need to break the latch because the gate was unlocked—surprising, since it meant that the electric security system was disarmed. Victor passed through the courtyard, where water splashed in the fountain, and mounted the stairs to the priest's apartment. He found the door ajar. Suspicious, he hesitated before bursting through the door. One lamp glowed in the empty living room. He found the kitchen and bedroom empty too, though lights were on in both rooms.

He left the apartment and headed to the cathedral, but when he reached the cathedral's side door, he sensed that the priest and Kyle were not inside. He didn't bother going in. They must have learned by now that he had fed on the priest's brother. Perhaps they were with the boy, fearful that Victor would attack again.

Victor traveled the few blocks to the Marigny, stopping outside the house of the priest's family. The lights were on. Had the priest gathered his family, intending to protect them all with the special powers granted to him?

Victor climbed the steps of the sloping porch of the house, illuminated by a yellow lightbulb. He turned the knob of the front door and found it unlocked. He flung it open. The long hallway lay in shadow, but light spilled out from the room at the end. As Victor approached it, the floor creaked under his weight. But not a sound stirred within. From the scent of blood, however, he knew the room was occupied. Fearless, he stepped in and discovered

Charles seated on a sofa, next to his dark-headed brother. Charles wore a clerical shirt and Roman collar. Kyle stood near a window. He was also dressed in black, like a priestly novice who still had not earned the white band for his throat, as though he was not yet quite worthy to don the old uniform once again. The brother stared at Victor fearfully, like a scared child. He wore a hooded green sweatshirt, the long strings dangling down the front. The room held an armchair and recliner, as well as a large-screen TV.

"How disappointing," Victor said. "I expected some attempt at resistance."

"Why?" Charles said, leaning forward on the sofa, as though ready to spring up if necessary. "You can't hurt us."

Kyle eyed Victor uncertainly, apparently not as confident as Charles of their safety.

Amused, Victor laughed. With a whim to tease his prey before pouncing, he moved into the room and sat in the armchair facing the sofa. "Do you really think the power protecting you extends to him?" Victor nodded at Pete.

"I can protect him!" Charles retorted.

"Really? You've seen the marks on his throat. You can't stay at his side every moment." Victor smiled wickedly at Pete, who looked deathly pale. The flavor of the boy's cool, salty throat was memorable. And he craved him now.

"Why don't you leave us alone, Victor?" Kyle suddenly pleaded. "Please, free me."

Victor glared at him. "And how might I do that? How might I free a thrall, who cannot live apart from me?"

"But I *can*," Kyle asserted with confidence, his gray eyes fixed on Victor. "I can feed on you whenever I want."

Victor laughed, dismissing Kyle's claim. But as his thrall continued staring earnestly, at him, Victor grew troubled. He drew up the sleeve of his silk shirt—more than enough clothing for a chilly body immune to more cold—and examined his forearm. Yes, he perceived a subtle sign in the texture of his flesh, detectable only to him, that Kyle had indeed fed. The magnitude of the discovery struck Victor. In his entire existence, no thrall had ever dared to take nourishment into his own hands. And even if a thrall had been so bold, Victor's own will would have prevented the liberty. Now, with his increased strength, his will should have been even more potent against such a liberty. How had this happened?

Furious, he sprang from the chair and lunged at Charles. The priest raised his arms in defense and managed to thrust Victor away and get to his feet. The priest's expression became fierce and his eyes showed a consciousness of a surging power within him. He suddenly came at Victor, clutching him by the throat.

Victor should have been prepared, but the strength of the attack surprised him. Only an equal stood a chance with him, as Paul had in his angry moments, but even Paul, fully a vampire, could not match Victor's level of strength. The priest tightened the grip on Victor's throat, immobilizing him. Charles's brown eyes, so fierce as he attacked, now became strangely vacant, as though the priest's consciousness had departed from his body and another force inhabited it. Victor's heart raced. He was not in danger of dying by strangulation. The means of destroying one like him were limited to the ways defined in vampire lore—a stake through the heart, exposure to full sunlight, a few lesser-known means. Still, he was stunned. It was as though a spider had spun a web around his thoughts. Nothing was clear. His only hope was the familiar one, to summon the violence that always lay just beneath the surface of his skin.

Gritting his teeth, he shoved Charles with his whole might.

Charles flew against the window above the sofa, shattering the glass. Charles's brother jumped up, staring first at Charles, then at Victor, but it was too late to flee. Victor fell on him, plunging his fangs into the boy's soft throat, then lapping the oozing blood. But suddenly he felt Charles's powerful hands on his shoulders. He felt himself being ripped away from his victim and flung against the floor.

He rose up with full force to face Charles, who stood between him and the boy. The boy still lay on the floor, trembling like a drug addict.

"You can't be with him every minute," Victor said, his chest heaving. "He's mine."

"No," Kyle suddenly blurted. He stood next to Charles, more livid than ever, his eyes scintillating. "I'll go back with you. Just leave them alone."

"I don't want you," Victor snapped. "I loved you. And you betrayed me." The potency of his feelings surprised Victor. Saying the words awakened him to the full extent of their truth. He realized now how deeply he had longed for Kyle to consent to the transformation that would make them equals. He looked from Kyle to Charles. "I'd rather have you always guessing. Who next? How? You can never protect them. And you won't forget that."

Victor stormed from the room and out the front door. Determined to vent his rage, he lifted into the night sky and flew to the Quarter. Landing in an alley, he pounced on a derelict relieving himself against a brick wall. Victor tore at his throat and drank until the man's heart slowed almost to the point of death, at which point he abandoned the victim, lest he doom himself by drinking from a corpse. Victor attacked two more men in the Quarter's dark streets, leaving them nearly dead, too. Finally satisfied, he soared to an abandoned plantation he knew of, twenty miles from New Orleans. He wanted solitude to brood.

He lighted on the damp earth, which sank beneath his steps. The decrepit mansion rose before him, a skeleton of cedar timbers and columns. He trod inside, avoiding holes in the rotting floor, and sat near the stone hearth, peering through the glassless window. At moments throughout his nocturnal life, his solitary existence became unbearable. This was such a moment. The heaviness of it made him wonder if now was finally the time for him to take his place in the Dark Kingdom. He was free to ascend. He had created another vampire—a vampire who might love him still and someday join him in the Dark Kingdom. He could ascend this very moment.

But was he willing to give up his plans? He had grown in strength as a vampire maker, and his power would increase with every new vampire he made. The Dark Kingdom might equip humans like Charles to fight him, but there was no evidence that they could assist a thrall, completely under his power. Kyle had taken nourishment without Victor's consent, but such a liberty was a far cry from the ability to harm his creator. Kyle might not be lost to Victor yet. The thrall's resistance must have its bounds. And if it didn't, he could destroy Kyle and create other thralls, many others. And from them he would eventually find willing partners for his scheme.

The thought of his growing strength consoled him when he considered the loss of Kyle. And yet . . . he felt his heart breaking.

He lay back on the rotting floor, feeling the humid air weighing on him like a damp blanket, and remembered a night not long after he and Kyle had first arrived in New Orleans. They lay naked on their sheets, Kyle's head on Victor's arm. For the first time, Kyle's lovemaking had been passionate without the compulsiveness he had dragged with him from his earthly life, when repression kept his desires in check until they rebelled and drove him to a quick fix followed by confession.

"I wish this could last forever," Kyle had said, stroking Victor's chest.

"No need to wish for what has already been granted you," Victor had answered. "Your past is just that. It's behind you. Leave it there."

They rested contentedly in silence for some time.

Then Kyle said, "I've never been to Rome. Could we go there?"

"Of course."

"We can go anywhere we want, can't we?" Kyle spoke as if the realization had just come to him.

"And whenever we want. Today. A thousand years from now."

"But it has to end sometime."

"Eternity doesn't end. I shouldn't have to tell you that, of all people. You preached it from the pulpit."

"That was another kind of eternity. But maybe the two eternal realms are linked. Maybe God allows them to coexist."

"Think what you want if it makes you happy."

"Will Jesus ever appear to me? Joshu, I mean."

"I'll ask him the next time I see him."

Victor closed his eyes now. He tried to shut out thoughts of Joshu and thoughts of Kyle. He tried to focus on the sense of triumph that would one day replace his every longing for love. But his efforts brought no comfort.

8

I'm to blame, Pete. There's no way around it." Charles looked out the window in Pete's bedroom. There was nothing to see but the clapboard wall of the house next door, five feet away, fading in the twilight. But he couldn't help wanting to watch for any sign of danger, for any sign of Victor.

"That's bull!" Pete said. He stretched out on the mattress, his hands behind his head. "It's not your fault. How could you know? I mean, how could you?"

Charles glanced at his brother, who was calmly gazing up at him. Pete wore a plaid shirt and blue jeans with a hole in the left knee. He seemed paler than usual, but otherwise he looked like his old self, the sparkle back in his dark eyes.

"Right," Charles chuckled grimly. "How could I know that a vampire would do such a thing? Can you believe this, Pete? A vampire."

They'd spent the past two evenings talking about Victor, with Pete trying to absorb Charles's explanation of Victor's history, of the Dark Kingdom, of Kyle's nature. Charles had described the horrifying encounter in the mausoleum. Pete needed little convincing, not with the wounds on his throat and his own undeniable experience of Victor's power. For two nights, Charles had slept on the floor on a blanket next to Pete's bed to protect his brother, getting up often in the night to check on his parents. He left the house before they got up so he wouldn't have to explain why he'd slept there.

Charles finally pulled himself away from the window. He was tired from two sleepless nights. He pulled the chair out from the desk, turned it toward Pete, and sat down.

"You can't guard me forever, you know," Pete said, turning his head toward his brother. "And what about Kyle? He's all alone at your apartment. What if Victor does decide to hurt him?"

Kyle had been staying in the apartment since the encounter with Victor the other night. Where else could he go? "Victor won't hurt him," Charles said confidently.

"You mean because of his plans for the two of them?" Pete said.

Charles nodded. He'd told Pete about Victor's efforts to persuade Kyle to join him as a predator of the night.

"But if Kyle keeps resisting, won't Victor finally hurt him? Can't he do that? Force him to become a vampire?"

"I told you, it has to be a free choice." Charles rubbed his eyes. He knew he needed to sleep. He should stretch out on the floor right now. But he was too wired to rest.

Pete sat up in the bed, leaning back against the wall to face Charles. "You care a lot about him, don't you?"

"Of course. You would, too, if you'd seen the two of them together. He's under Victor's thumb." Charles realized he sounded defensive. The question had made him uncomfortable. He tried to reassure himself that Pete only meant that Charles was a good friend, but it didn't help. His nerves were still taut.

"But they're lovers. Maybe that's why Victor has so much control."

"They're not lovers anymore!" Charles snapped, full of jealousy at the thought of Kyle still clinging to Victor. He was surprised at strength of his feelings. He couldn't deny them any longer. He regretted lashing out his brother. "Sorry, Pete," he said. "I have a confession to make. I think I'm in love with Kyle."

"In love?" Pete looked puzzled.

Charles nodded, ashamed. "I thought I was cured. I realized what my orientation was back in high school. I got kind of wild in college. Lots of weekends at the bars and sleeping around."

"You never told Mom and Dad?" Pete looked surprised, but his gaze showed no hint of judgment.

"No. And, of course, you were too young to tell that I was queer." Charles sighed, relieved that he'd opened up. "Then my senior year in college, something happened."

As Charles described the apparition of Christ, his own promise, and his therapy sessions, Pete listened intently, straining to take everything in, but clearly believing Charles and feeling for him.

Finally concluding his story, Charles sighed. "But maybe God is just testing me with these feelings. If I resist them, maybe they'll disappear once and for all."

"That's bull, Charles," Pete said, suddenly adamant. "There's nothing wrong with your feelings. There's nothing to be cured of! How can you think that?"

"I have to think that, Pete." His brother's response surprised Charles. He had no idea Pete was capable of dismissing Church teaching. "I'm a Catholic priest."

"Bullshit!" Pete scooted to the edge of the bed, lowering his feet to the floor. He gazed intently at Charles. "If that's who you are, it's who you are. We don't live in the Stone Age. For Chrissake, Charles!"

Charles was too tired to argue. He smiled at his brother,

grateful for the attempt to defend him, and shook his head. "I'm exhausted. I've gotta sack out."

He got up and spread a blanket on the floor. He stretched out on it, kicking off his shoes.

"Here," Pete said, handing Charles his pillow. "You need it worse than I do."

Charles smiled and placed the pillow under his head. A moment later he was asleep.

After five uneventful nights, Charles returned to his apartment in the evenings. Kyle had assured him that, as a thrall, he sensed Victor's movements and would know if Victor approached Pete's house in the Marigny—in time for Charles to intervene. And Charles knew he couldn't continue indefinitely playing the sentinel. He prayed to God that Pete would be okay.

Kyle continued staying at Charles's apartment, sleeping on the sofa at night. Charles thought that Kyle's separation from Victor seemed to give Kyle a new sense of strength. His desperation seemed to dwindle. He comforted Charles, praying with him, encouraging him to lose himself in his parish duties. It was as though he'd discovered a new sense of purpose and forgotten Victor.

Late one night, when Charles had gotten up to use the bathroom, he found Kyle sitting peacefully on the balcony.

"Can't sleep?" Charles said. Wearing boxers and a T-shirt, he hugged himself in the chilly air and sat next to Kyle.

"Look at the moon."

A full orange moon rose straight overhead.

They both gazed in silence.

"Thank you for rescuing me," Kyle said. "And for not blaming me for what Victor did to Pete."

Charles nodded in acknowledgment. He felt a surge of tenderness for Kyle. He wanted more than anything to take him in his arms.

"I go to the cemetery every day, to feed," Kyle said, his eyes still on the moon. "And when I'm standing over Victor, the same thought comes to my head. I think it's the voice of God. Save him! That's what it says. Save him!"

"How can you save Victor?"

Kyle hesitated. "By taking his life."

The suggestion—or, rather, its coming from Kyle—shocked Charles. "Taking his life! And sending him to hell?"

Kyle shook his head. He turned to Charles, his gaze full of earnestness. "He won't go to hell. He's in hell now. If he dies, God will take him to heaven. That's what I keep hearing God say. 'I'll claim him as my own. He'll be with me in Paradise.' Killing him is not like killing a human being. He's not human anymore. He's like Satan on the earth. And I'm like his consort. I can save him and myself."

An alarm went off in Charles's head. He grabbed Kyle's arm. "You mean end your own life! You can't do that. Ending his life means ending yours."

Kyle smiled tranquilly. "I'm ready to end this kind of existence."

"Don't say that!" Charles tightened his grip on Kyle. "Even if you wanted to, you can't. Your nature won't let you allow harm to come to Victor."

"That's why you have to do it."

"Me? I've already tried. You stopped me, and you'll stop me again."

"I was acting instinctively then. Like a mother bear protecting her cub. If I intentionally prepare for it, if I kneel before the

Blessed Sacrament while you do it, Christ will give me strength to resist. Christ has that power. We both believe it."

"The Joshu that Victor loved? He can't want to destroy Victor."

Kyle shook his head. "Not destroy. Save. Christ has been speaking to my heart. I know it."

Charles was unconvinced—these were all hypotheticals. And the idea of entering the tomb again was unbearable. "I couldn't make myself do it again."

"With Christ's help, you could!" Kyle leaned toward him, his face inches from Charles's. His eyes were lovely in the moonlight, so boyish and innocent. "If you do this, I'll be free," Kyle continued softly. "I know it in my heart. Every sphere is under God's power. I couldn't see it before. My faith was weak. But now I know. God won't allow any of his own to perish. If you end Victor's existence as it is, I'll be free."

"You mean you'll die." Charles could barely speak the words.

"No. I'll go back to my human life the way it was. Victor is deceived. His vision is distorted. You have to believe that, too. You're a priest. We're both priests."

Charles felt lightheaded, confused—like an infatuated schoolgirl. He released his hold on Kyle and sat back. "I don't know."

"Do it for your brother's sake."

This brought Charles back to himself. "You said you'd know if Victor approached Pete. I could intercept him."

"But what if this power of yours disappears? Then what?"

The thought horrified Charles. Kyle was right. What if the power left him? He stared down at the fountain in the courtyard. He felt like running to Pete, making sure he was safe in his bed.

"Don't worry," Kyle said, as though he could read Charles's

thoughts. "Victor will take his time. That way he has leverage over us."

"Maybe. But we can't be sure."

Kyle did not refute him.

A sense of solemn inevitability settled like a weight on Charles. Kyle was right. "I have to do it soon."

Kyle nodded.

They sat and stared silently into the night. Charles knew he had to think through the logistics of a second trip to the mausoleum. But he couldn't do it now. He had to sleep. Maybe he would see everything more clearly in the morning. He went back to his room and crawled under the sheets.

He had barely drifted off, when a sensation of falling made his body jerk.

Once again he had the sense of a presence in the room. His eyes flashed open. He scanned the darkness. Something fell to the floor. He switched on the lamp by his bed and got up to survey the room. On the floor by his dresser was a framed photograph of his parents taken at the party thrown to celebrate their twenty-fifth wedding anniversary five years ago. He picked it up. His mother wore a pale blue dress, a little cross dangling from her throat on a chain. His father was in a navy blazer and white shirt, open at the collar. They stood over a cake with candles formed like the number 25. A diagonal crack in the glass crossed through their bodies. A sense of foreboding rose in Charles. He thrashed in his bed the rest of the night, barely sleeping at all.

As Charles said Mass and visited parishioners the next day, Kyle's horrible request continued to weigh on him. He started to pour out his soul to Dr. Beauchamp that evening at his weekly session after he passed his plethysmograph test with flying colors—too distracted to feel the least arousal.

"This is so horrible," Dr. Beauchamp said when Charles had finished his account of Victor's attack on Pete. She was swathed in royal blue. Silver earrings with lapis lazuli in them dangled from her ears. "The violence of it . . ." Her brow furrowed in sympathy, and she shook her head. "And this—Kyle is his name?—he's staying with you? He's afraid that Victor will hurt him?"

"I don't think he is. Victor didn't threaten him. I think Victor really wants him back."

"He must not go back," Dr. Beauchamp said firmly. "It would be best for him to leave New Orleans. For his own safety."

"It's not that easy." Charles explained Kyle's need, amazed that he could report the feeding ritual of thralls so matter-of-factly.

Dr. Beauchamp listened placidly, not a trace of incredulity in her expression. "I think there's another issue you haven't acknowledged. You clearly do not want Kyle to leave."

Charles felt the blood rush to his face, as if he were a little boy caught playing with himself. "No," he admitted, "I don't."

"You think you're in love with him."

"I am in love with him."

"Infatuation feels very much like love. This is the moment of testing for you. Perhaps God has sent Kyle to test you."

"Yes. I believe that."

"What else could it be? You must not take these feelings seriously. And yet . . ."

"What?"

"There's something in your reluctance to send Kyle away. If this is a test, then perhaps you must carry it out to the end. Let Kyle remain with you, platonically. If you resist temptation in such close quarters, you will resist it in the future, no matter how strong it may be."

Charles felt confused. He wanted nothing more than to let Kyle stay with him. But wouldn't that be like tempting God? "The Act of Contrition says to avoid the nearer occasion of sin," he said.

Anger flashed in Dr. Beauchamp's eyes for the first time since Charles had begun therapy with her. "I don't need to be reminded of the prayers of our faith," she said. "But also recall the scripture passage from Ecclesiastes: 'For everything there is a season, and a time for every matter under heaven.' There's a time to flee temptation and a time to confront it, head on."

"I don't know," Charles said doubtfully. "I don't think I'm strong enough."

"Of course, you aren't. But divine power is another matter. Trust it."

Charles nodded, sighing. His gaze drifted to an ebony carving of an African tribesman raising a machete, one of the many art pieces on the shelves lining one wall. "There's something else," he said.

Dr. Beauchamp looked at him expectantly.

"You probably won't believe it."

"Perhaps not. But go on."

"Kyle wants me to destroy Victor."

"Destroy him?" Dr. Beauchamp looked alarmed.

"You don't believe he's not human. You think I'd be committing murder. You're wrong, Doctor. I shouldn't have told you." Charles started to stand.

"Wait! Please. I'm trying to understand. If Victor is what you claim, and Kyle as well, then why would Kyle want you to kill the one he depends upon? Killing Victor means killing Kyle."

"Kyle doesn't think so. He believes that he'll be free if I kill Victor. He'll become his old self, and Victor will be saved."

"Saved!" Dr. Beauchamp chuckled. "How can a vampire be saved?"

Charles could hardly blame Beauchamp for not believing him. He could barely believe his own words.

"I'm just trying to understand," Dr. Beauchamp explained. She seemed to search the air for the right words. "You're right. This is all hard to believe. But as I've told you, I don't doubt the dark powers of the universe. I don't doubt that Victor and his protégé inhabit a dangerous, sacrilegious realm. I'm only afraid that if you resort to this kind of violence, you will enter their unholy world. There will be blood on your hands."

"But I'm already in their world," Charles said, feeling desperate.

"No. You're not. You rescued Victor's protégé from it. Don't give up on him. Especially not to ease your own fears of falling from divine favor. That would be selfish."

"Maybe you're right." He couldn't send Kyle to his ruin just to spare himself from attractions he didn't want to fight. Who escaped the battle of good and evil?

When the session ended, Dr. Beauchamp did something she had never done before. She stood over Charles, with her hands upon his head, uttering a prayer in a language he did not understand. It might have been Greek, except for all the gutteral sounds. She didn't give him the opportunity to inquire about it. After the prayer, she raised her finger to her lips and led him to the front door in silence, as though speaking might ruin the prayerful atmosphere.

As he unchained his Vespa only steps from Dr. Beauchamp's door, a sudden, deep laugh startled him. He turned to find Victor studying him, his arms folded, his white face luminous in the darkness.

"What words of wisdom did she bestow on you, this mentor of yours?" Victor's teeth, bright and livid, flashed as he spoke.

Charles did not back away. "What do you want?"

"She's the one who gave you strength. Not your god. I should know. I know her power well. It made me what I am."

"She's a psychologist. She's got nothing to do with you." Charles worried that he had endangered Dr. Beauchamp by leading Victor to her.

"I saw her in the cathedral. Protecting you. I didn't recognize her then. But now it's all clear. How does it feel to be surrounded by darkness, Father? In every direction. With no hope of escape."

"I can escape you. So can Kyle."

Victor studied him with amusement. Then he turned, and casting a glance at the shuttered window of Beauchamp's office, disappeared into the darkness.

Shaken, Charles climbed the stairs to Beauchamp's door and rang the bell. When Dr. Beauchamp appeared, he told her about the encounter. He said he was worried that Victor might try to hurt her.

She shook her head, calmly. "He won't."

"How can you be so sure? I should stay with you."

"There is no need. Please, don't worry." Beauchamp closed the door without another word.

Reluctantly, Charles climbed down the steps and boarded his motorbike. On the drive to his parents' house he mulled over Victor's words about seeing Dr. Beauchamp in the cathedral, about her protection of him. None of it made sense. He decided to dismiss his fears. Why should he believe anything Victor said? Victor only wanted to torment him and Kyle.

Charles spent the evening with his parents and Pete, looking at family photos. It felt good to laugh over photos of Pete as a toddler, peeing in the middle of the yard, smiling without his front teeth on his First Communion day. And photos of Charles's ordination day reminded him of his calling, and the strength that came with it.

It was after ten when Charles said goodnight. Instead of riding directly home, where Kyle awaited him, he headed to the cathedral. Inside the dark church he knelt at the communion rail, his eyes fixed on the flickering sanctuary candle, encased in red glass. Maybe it was a sin to test God, but he asked for a sign. *You've spoiled me, God. You got me expecting apparitions. Let me know what I'm supposed to do.*

He knelt there for nearly an hour, trying to listen for an answer. But inevitably his mind wandered to Kyle. He'd never felt the way he felt about Kyle. The excitement of sexual attraction he knew, but never attraction and tenderness. This was a harder feeling to fight. It didn't *seem* dirty. He imagined the two of them sharing a refurbished shotgun in the Quarter, sitting side by side in the evenings on a sofa, a big, friendly dog at their feet. He imagined making love, kissing Kyle on the forehead and chest and belly.

Suddenly he sensed someone in the sanctuary. He shot to his feet and found himself once again facing Victor, who stood near the altar. He didn't bother asking how Victor entered the locked church. Victor approached him. Charles's eyes had adjusted to the darkness, and he stared into Victor's face, barely a foot away from his own.

"I don't know what he's told you," Victor continued. "He can continue feeding as he has been only as long as I allow it."

"You have no choice."

"You mean because of your power? You can't protect him."

"Don't be so sure."

"But I am sure. I created him and I can destroy him."

"You want him back. You wouldn't destroy him!"

Victor stepped closer, his eyes only inches from Charles's own. "You know nothing of what I will or won't do, for all your power. And I'm willing to wager that you're more vulnerable to me than you think."

Charles felt Victor's breath on his face. He felt lightheaded, and a warm flood seemed to rush through his body. He felt himself moving toward Victor's lips. His groin tingled and his legs weakened. Victor embraced him. Victor's parted lips met his. Though they were cool, they made Charles feverish. *What are you doing?* A voice inside his head seemed to warn him, but he was powerless to resist Victor. Were they sinking to the marble floor? Was Victor nuzzling his throat? Was he burrowing his body into Charles's? Charles had never felt so intoxicated, surrendering so utterly to another person.

When his mind cleared, he lay on the sanctuary floor. There was no sign of Victor, but his body continued to glow with Victor's touch. So Victor was right. The strange power with which he'd fended off Victor's attack had not protected him from Victor's seductive force. A fear suddenly rose in him. He touched his throat, probing it for wounds. There were none.

He felt a sense of shame for desiring such a monster. Was it Victor's intention to win back Kyle by making him jealous? Charles could understand nothing.

Disoriented, lethargic, he left the cathedral and returned to his apartment. He found Kyle in the living room, calmly reading.

"Did you feed today?" Charles said, sitting next to Kyle on the sofa.

"Yes. My last time."

Charles shook his head. "I don't know if I can do it."

"You have to," Kyle said firmly, his gray eyes placid.

"Why kill him? Why not just run away?"

"You know why."

Charles contemplated a rosy watercolor of the Spanish Steps on the wall across from them. He'd bought it from an artist on the Piazza Navona in Rome, while he was studying theology. He took Kyle's hand in his. "I'm in love with you," he said.

Kyle pulled his hand away. "All the more reason to do this."

"Do you feel the same?" Charles watched Kyle's profile expectantly.

Kyle's expression revealed nothing. He stared ahead, his white-blond hair curling behind his ear. "I can't. I'll be lost if I do."

Charles felt disappointed. But he knew he should feel relieved. His dangerous feelings were a moot concern.

"Promise me, you'll do it." Kyle turned to him now.

"I promise."

Charles tossed and turned all night. He finally got up at dawn and stepped into the living room. Kyle was sleeping peacefully on the sofa. He lay on his side, his strong bare arm outside the blue blanket. Charles left him there, dressed, and went out for coffee to let Kyle sleep. He worked in the office all morning, glancing out the window from time to time at his apartment. At eleven thirty, he saw Kyle emerge and walk down the gallery to the stairs. He was dressed all in black. As he crossed the courtyard, he glanced up and saw Charles. He hesitated for a moment before continuing toward the gate. Charles knew he was on the way to the cathedral, to pray for strength while Charles carried out his promise.

Charles picked up his backpack, which held the tools he

needed, and descended to the Vespa parked in the courtyard. The day was cloudy and cool, and as he rode through the French Quarter to the Garden District, a fine drizzle fell on this face and hands.

He arrived at Lafayette only minutes before noon, but there was no sign of the caretaker who locked the gates. His feet seemed to be made of stone as he walked through the tombs to Victor's grave. *God help me. God help me. God help me.* The words were like a solemn drumbeat in his head.

In front of the Greek façade of Victor's tomb, he froze, his eyes fixed on the name Boudreaux, inscribed above the iron door. Finally, he retrieved the nutpick from his backpack and inserted it in the keyhole. His hands were sweaty and fumbling, and he dropped the pick. He snatched it up and once again inserted it, maneuvering it until the lock clicked. He opened the door wide, dispelling the darkness from Victor's casket. He took a step, then stopped. What if Kyle was wrong? What if Kyle couldn't survive without Victor? And what if destroying Victor sent him to hell? As much as Charles wanted revenge for the attacks on Pete, he couldn't send Victor to eternal damnation.

He stepped back out of the mausoleum and shut the door. The wind rustled the magnolias as he stood, trying to collect himself.

"Hey, closing time!"

The caretaker, an old man in a ball cap, pointed to his watch.

Charles nodded and made for the gate.

He rode directly to the cathedral and found Kyle inside, kneeling in the front pew. He genuflected before the tabernacle and entered the pew, kneeling by Kyle. Not far from them, a woman in a flowered scarf lit a votive candle. Charles waited for her to leave before he spoke.

"I tried, but I couldn't."

Dejected, Kyle sank back against the pew. "No wonder it was so easy to stay here. Victor was never in danger."

"Come on," Charles said. "Let's go eat something."

Kyle shook his head, and Charles left him.

That evening, he went to bed early and fell asleep immediately. In the night he woke up in alarm to see someone standing over him. Was it Victor? He sat up, ready to fight him.

Then he saw that it was Kyle. Kyle crawled under the sheets. He wrapped his arms around Charles. Charles kissed him tenderly on the lips. Kyle began working off Charles's briefs. His heart pounding with excitement, Charles let him, casting his own vow of celibacy to the wind.

9

The house on Rampart, quiet and modest, seemed innocent enough, but a strange suspicion had led Victor to follow the priest here earlier in the evening, and with his ability to hear even whispers behind walls when he attuned his ears to them, he had heard *her* voice. She was affecting some kind of accent, but the familiar intonations were unmistakable. Now Victor was back to confront her.

As he approached the front door, the wind gusted, scuttling a crumpled paper bag down the sidewalk. He tried the door. It was not locked. He opened it and entered a dark hallway. He slowly advanced toward a room at the back of the house, aglow with flickering light. When he reached the room, he discovered the source of the illumination: hundreds of candles burned on tables and shelves and a fireplace mantle, under which a fire crackled. The black walls were like the sky of a moonless night. Two enormous chairs, draped in velvet, faced the fireplace. A shower of dreadlocks fell over the back of one of the chairs.

"Welcome, Victor," she said.

Though two millennia had passed since he'd heard it, he recognized it instantly, as a child would recognize the voice of its mother. And, indeed, the woman who spoke was a mother of sorts. Victor walked around the chair and stood before her.

"Tiresia," he said.

"Victor." She sat ensconced like a queen, her arms resting on the arms of the chair, her chin up. She was robed in diamond-studded purple. A thick necklace of diamonds lay on her bosom, above a scooped neckline. Her brown skin, stretched over high cheekbones, gleamed in the firelight.

"Two thousand years. And you are just as captivating."

"And you. I can see why I chose you."

"But you didn't," Victor said. "You followed your own maker to the Dark Kingdom. You didn't expect me to pledge my devotion to you and follow you when the allotted time passed."

"No. But I enjoyed your beauty for a moment. You were my last lusty affair."

"If you call a single mounting an affair." Victor recalled with delight his wanton intercourse with Tiresia after he had siphoned blood from her breast, and then with revulsion the shriveled brown corpse she had become, like a giant bladder of an animal, before turning to dust. "It's good to see that your beauty was not destroyed after all."

Tiresia smiled. "You should have known that. I showed you a vision of the Dark Kingdom. Do you remember a single example of ugliness there?"

He could see where she was directing the conversation. "So now, you've become an emissary of the Dark Kingdom." Victor sat on a settee facing her. "The authorities must be desperate."

"Can you think of a better emissary? How can you deny your maker?"

"My maker neglected to tell me how much power comes with violating the rules. You must envy me. I've created another of my kind and remained in this sphere with him, my equal, my lover."

"Oh? I don't see him. Where is he?"

Victor brushed off her attempt to provoke him. "You know me, Tiresia, even from our limited encounters in your Jerusalem hovel. I'm not one to pledge my love for eternity. Variety is better. I can move from lover to lover across the globe, populating it with my creations, beings like me."

Tiresia made a face to show she wasn't impressed. "No, threaten all you want. You long for love. You always have. Your life as a vampire began because of spurned love. And over the centuries I have watched you searching for a replacement for him. But you'll never find one. The moment you create another being like you, you'll be forced to part from him—if you want him to survive. As you well know, the Dark Kingdom loves its own, but it will destroy even its own to protect the freedom of our sphere. Violations freeze our life. The order of the cosmos won't allow them. So no matter how often you violate them, you will always be forced to surrender the fruits of your transgression."

"I don't believe you. My power has increased since I created another vampire. For the first time in two thousand years, I have seen the twilight."

"You're foolish. The twilight for you is like the light that mortals see before they die. I'm warning you, Victor." The pride and amusement that had played in Tiresia's dark eyes on reuniting with her fierce creation now vanished. She stared gravely at him. "You've transformed one who will gladly follow you to the Dark Kingdom two centuries from now, when his allotted time is over. You'll have everything you want. An eternity of bliss in the sphere where you belong and an eternal consort."

"Four years have passed. You think I still long for Paul?"

"Don't tell me you long for this pathetic thrall of yours."

"When he's transformed, you won't say that about him."

"I see." Tiresia reflected for a moment and appeared to embark on a new tactic. "You know, what you saw two thousand years ago when I transported you through time and space was not an illusion. Your vision of the Dark Kingdom was not merely a vision. It was reality. A new, invigorated Rome, with grand palaces and gymnasiums. With lush gardens and seasons that are always mild, suitable for casting off all garments to walk arm in arm with a lovely creature of your choice, to make love on the lawns or in the middle of a chariot arena. Feasting, lovemaking, athletics, laughter. Life, Victor—movement, growth, excitement. And a unique brand of life, one that never grows old, or tired, or discontent. What you saw as we soared together over that sphere is magnificent. And what do you have here in this existence? Perpetual darkness, imprisonment within a tomb—always vulnerable to the merest child who desires your destruction by day."

Victor stared at her, unmoved by her description. "Yes. And why do you care about danger to my existence?"

"You're wrong to believe that beings like us have no sympathy for one another. Don't judge by your own hard nature. You acquired that long before you became what you are now."

"It has served me well."

Tiresia shrugged. "Perhaps. But perhaps it will be your downfall."

"Your motives are selfish. My life here disturbs your life there. That's all."

"I admit it. The laws of the universe forbid the association of vampires on the earth. All predators serve a purpose in the food chain, as modern scientists have called it. But a concentration of predators disturbs the cosmic order, and when the order is disturbed there are repercussions. Inhabitants of the Dark Kingdom are punished for your violation. Our life is frozen until ambassadors like me persuade violators to desist. Still, we love our own. We destroy those like us only as a last resort. Because when we do destroy, we experience a collective pain. We grieve."

"But life there is not frozen. I agreed to leave the vampire I created. The Dark Kingdom was appeased. You move freely now."

"True. And now you would freeze life once more by creating another vampire."

Victor laughed. "You're not here on the same mission that brought Sonia to me. There's something else. My power. I'm a vampire maker now. The more vampires I create, the more powerful I'll become. You fear a rival realm."

"You think you are the only vampire maker that's ever existed!" retorted Tiresia, angry now. "There have been others. But you won't find one alive any longer. Travel the earth. See for yourself. Don't delude yourself into believing you can ever initiate a realm to rival that of the Dark Kingdom. If you want to test us, be my guest. But why risk your own life?"

"You would rather take his life first. My thrall's. Wouldn't you? So what have I to lose?"

Tiresia nodded, sizing Victor up. "You are hard, indeed."

Victor continued, without responding to her observation. "Yet I'm not so sure your authority extends over my thrall. He's my creation. He doesn't belong to your sphere."

Tiresia said nothing.

Victor grinned. "I see it's true. You can do nothing until his transformation, which will happen only with his consent. Even I can't force him. You see, I do acknowledge my limitations. And once he has consented and has undergone transformation, he is one of our kind. Then you face the same dilemma you face in me, unless of course the more ancient of us are worth more to those in the Dark Kingdom than the fledglings. But whatever you do, I will have increased my power as a vampire maker. That frightens you. Perhaps your concern rests less with the cosmic order than with your own pride. You and the other inhabitants of the Dark Kingdom see yourselves as gods. Then I must be your Prometheus, stealing your fire to illuminate my own world."

Tiresia raised her chin in indignation. "You look above and see only your own reflection."

"Oh, no. I'm not deluded. I look at you and see one who covets power. I know why you didn't beg me to pledge myself to you before you entered the Dark Kingdom. I've had two thousand years to reflect on it. You fear having an equal."

"Why should I have wanted you as a lover? I had a lover awaiting me."

"I don't believe you."

Tiresia laughed heartily. "I think I see. You feel spurned. Oh Victor, it's always been the same with you. Beneath all your roaring beats a tender heart. Love is all you've ever wanted. But you'll never have it, as perhaps you've heard from another authority. Because you don't know the difference between love and power. Neither do I, but I've never pretended to want love."

"What authority do you refer to?" Victor said, stung by a sense of violation. How could she know of Joshu and his realm?

Tiresia shrugged. She picked up a palm frond, painted in bright Caribbean colors, and fanned her face.

He saw it was no use probing and returned to the subject of the Dark Kingdom's own authority. "And the priest? If you need him as your instrument it means you can't touch my thrall—not directly."

"What do I care what you think?"

Victor enjoyed seeing that the advantage was now his. "Yes, why should you?" he gloated. "But you must care what the priest thinks. Once he knows the real nature of Dr. Beauchamp, he's lost to your influence. Protect him all you want. I'll have no reason to harm him."

"You think he'll take *your* word? Listen to me, Victor." Tiresia moved forward on her chair. She tightened her hold on the arms and stared intently at him—earnestly, it seemed, since she could assume any attitude. "You have no use for the Dark Kingdom? Very well. You want to roam the earth for eternity? Then do it. Live like the predator you are. Enjoy your victims however you wish. Create thrall after thrall to do your bidding, to satisfy all of your lusts. You are determined to reign as the only ruler—and don't deceive yourself into believing that you would share your kingdom with an equal whom you create. You never, never will. Live the unchallenged power of your territory on the earth, but abandon this enterprise. I warn you, you will not win."

Victor mused for a long moment. "Why did the Dark Kingdom send you, Tiresia?"

Tiresia settled back in her chair. "It's obvious, isn't it? I created you. Our bond might convince you."

Victor laughed. "Our bond? I took you on the floor of your hovel in Jerusalem. I swallowed your blood. You shriveled to nothing. I confiscated the treasures you'd amassed over your centuries of existence. I never thought of you again. I never dreamed of you. Bond, indeed!"

"I can't believe it. You're trying to wound me. I'm flattered that you care enough to want me to suffer. And I admit, your words pierce me like arrows." The irony in Tiresia's throaty voice was strong. "Tell me the truth. I'm very curious. Has it been worth it for you? To live two millennia as you do. Haunted by him? Pursuing him. Seeking to replace him?"

Glaring at her, Victor said nothing.

"At times I wonder if he'll succeed. Can you believe that I even consider such a possibility? A being like you, capable of such malice, unyielding—for all of the human longings of your heart. How could he ever win you over? But no matter. There's no leaving one eternal realm for another. For all his promises, that is not possible. So he would win you over in vain."

Victor stood. "You're here in vain. I'll do what I want, as I want."

As he exited the room, he glanced back. Instead of beholding a beautiful African face, he beheld a hideous mask, the mouth open and fangs displayed. Tiresia hissed at him.

Until nearly dawn, he paced Rampart Street, reflecting on Tiresia's words. So she had observed from her own sphere his centuries of existence on the earth. She had watched his futile pursuit of Joshu. Was she telling the truth about the vanity of leaving one sphere for another? If so, why had Joshu bothered pleading with him over the centuries?

He had never wasted his time trying to understand the order of the spheres and their relationships to one another. Now, however, his interest was keen. He wondered just how much control these spheres exercised over him, how much power he could amass. Was it fear that he had beheld in Tiresia's eyes? Surely, the benevolence she claimed was merely a ruse. Since when did agents from the Dark Kingdom care whether creatures like him lived or died?

Standing in the shadows and willing himself to go undetected, he waited on the street until Tiresia emerged. Then he followed her to St. Louis Cemetery, just a block away. Effortlessly, she leapt over the wall. He did likewise, following her to a mausoleum in the center of the cemetery where she snapped open the gate and entered.

The first light of dawn threatened, but he still felt strong in his new power. Brazenly he followed her into the mausoleum. He felt the crypts on either side. Sensing her presence in a top berth, he pried off the marble tablet and laid it on the floor. She lay peacefully, her hands clasped beneath her breasts. The hideous mask had disappeared. Her luscious beauty once more shone placidly forth. While he peered down at her, she opened her eyes, but they stared up vacantly, as though drugs clouded her mind. His impulse was to kiss her, his lovely creator. But he also considered choking the life out of her—as if he could. Since she had passed from earth to another existence in the Dark Kingdom, he doubted that he could have the power to harm her. And what good would it do? The Dark Kingdom held a host of emissaries.

He replaced the stone and exited the mausoleum, securing the gate behind him. He lifted, moving through space at the speed of light, arms extended like the bats of vampire lore and sped to his own sleeping place. Light from the rising sun glowed strongly now, and even with his new level of power, his skin was beginning to sting. He hastened inside the mausoleum and crawled into his coffin. His last thoughts were of Tiresia's fascinating, dazed eyes.

He dreamed he lived in a Roman palace. He reclined on a couch in a room made of polished marble. The furniture was gilded. Opulent mirrors, framed in rubies and sapphires, magnified the grand chamber. A fountain gushed in the center, around the nude figure of a discus thrower, his body twisting in action. Victor stood up and moved to a window that looked down on an enormous courtyard aglow in torchlight. Vampires gathered around athletic victims in loincloths, each taking turns pressing their lips to wounded throats. When the vampires beheld him at the window, standing over them like the pope over St. Peter's Square, they released their victims, stood, and bowed profoundly in homage to him.

A palace of vampires. And beyond the palace walls—he knew— a kingdom of vampires. And he, the ruler of them all. Surely that kingdom would make him forget Joshu—or else would make Joshu's visits to plead with him all the more frequent.

Then he leaped from the window into the night sky and sped over the city to a lonely desert, lighting on rocky knoll overlooking an oasis. In a calm pool, glimmering in moonlight, Joshu bathed himself. He signaled for Victor to join him. Victor plunged headfirst from the hill, soaring down into the pool and rising up through the water. When he emerged, Joshu was nowhere in sight.

The following night, Victor ensconced himself in a high back rattan chair in the garden behind his house. The damp night lay heavily on the lush walls of ivy around him, on the philodendrons, hibiscuses, and nandinas dotted with red berries. The glass conservatory attached to the rear of the mansion rose before him, a jungle of tropical plants visible to his acute eyes through the dark glass.

He concentrated barely at all to summon his thrall, and within half an hour, Kyle wandered across the stones of the garden to Victor's rattan throne. He moved like a sleepwalker, having no choice but to answer Victor's call. If it had pleased Victor to have Kyle at his command in this somnambulant state, his thrall could never have fled from him. And in the early centuries of his existence, Victor would have been quite satisfied with such forced faithfulness. Now he wanted consent. He was not adverse to manipulating and seducing. He was certainly not adverse to punishing—even destroying. But the pleasure of domination now required a response that was in some real sense voluntary.

Zombielike, Kyle stood before him, awaiting his bidding. He was a lovely boy, solid and compact of figure, with the proportions of a gladiator of old—wide shoulders, thick throat, pectoral muscles that rode high beneath his black sweater. A twinge of longing rose in Victor, a bothersome twinge of emotional as well as physical attraction. He willed Kyle to full consciousness. The glazed look fell from his eyes. He stared fearfully at Victor now.

"You think I brought you here to destroy you?" Victor said. "I could have done that long ago. Sit." Victor motioned to the stone bench facing him.

Kyle obeyed.

Victor delighted to see that the fear in the thrall's eyes was owed as much to his own attraction to his maker as to his maker's purpose in bringing him here. But there was something more in Kyle's expression, something more in his fear.

"What do you have to confess?" Victor said.

"I asked him to destroy you." Kyle did not flinch.

Victor laughed. "Yes. I'm sure he would like to send me to hell. If he could."

"I'm telling the truth. I asked him to destroy you."

Victor surveyed Kyle's face. "Yes. I see you did. And how was he to do that, since he would be facing a thrall whose every instinct requires him to defend his master? How exactly did you propose to counter your own nature?"

"By prayer. While Charles went to your mausoleum, I was on my knees before the tabernacle. And he did, Victor. I didn't feel the slightest urge to save you. But Charles couldn't do it. He was afraid if he destroyed you, I would die, too."

"And so you would." Victor mused on this scenario. Perhaps Tiresia was telling the truth when she claimed that the Dark Kingdom loved its own. Perhaps she protected him as he lay sleeping in the tomb. And the power she had invested in Charles did not allow him to harm a vampire.

"And you were willing to die?" Victor finally said.

Kyle nodded solemnly. "To gain heaven."

"You're deluded. You don't belong to the sphere of heaven and hell. You belong to my sphere."

Kyle's somber determination vanished. He pounded the bench with both hands. "I don't belong anywhere!" he blurted. "I'm living in limbo. I'm not dead and I'm not alive. I'm not a consecrated priest, and I am. I want to kill you, and I want you to possess me."

"Yes," Victor said, a sense of triumph welling up within him. "There is only one way to peace. You know what it is."

"I don't believe you. Christ will never abandon me."

"Your Christ is irrelevant.

Kyle shook his head, his eyes filling with tears. "Please end this. Kill me so I can go to him."

"If you think you can go to Christ, why not end your own life?"

"You know I can't. I've tried. Your power won't let me do it."

"Don't blame it on my power."

"But it's true. If you'd let me do it, I would. If I can never go to heaven, then I can never go to hell. So I might as well go to oblivion. It's better than this."

Victor eyed him coolly. "If you think so, you're mad. Look what you have. Eternity. With a lover to spend it with. You'll never escape our world, so why not relish it? And if, after the required sojourn on this earth, you want to choose heaven for our own kind, so be it. If living as a predator offends your sensibilities, it need be for a limited time only. Of course, you'll find that after the transformation your sensibilities won't be so tender."

Kyle lowered his eyes despairingly. "That's what I'm afraid of."

"Think of it, Kyle. Power over all mortals. Power over who lives and who dies. Power to equal my own. I'll no longer be your master."

Kyle lifted his face. "You would really give that up? I can't believe it."

"You forget. I've done it before. Why not again?"

"You loved Paul before you made him what you are. It made the sacrifice easier."

The words opened a wound that Victor believed had finally healed. Paul Lewis, the sensuous artist, had indeed captivated him. He wondered for a moment what Paul was doing back on the east coast where Victor had left him, allowing him to believe that his lover had set off for the Dark Kingdom, in obedience to the powers that be. For Paul's safety, as much as for his own, he had parted. Now, perhaps Paul had taken another lover. Victor's pride forbade him to reveal his vulnerability to his thrall. "It was no sacrifice," he said. "His nature was equal to mine, but I knew I would always be more powerful than a neophyte. That would also be true with you."

"So, you don't love me at all? You only want to transform me to assert yourself against the Dark Kingdom. To increase your own power?"

"What of it? A million souls would do anything to have the life I'm offering you."

Kyle reflected a moment. His face glowed milky white in the moonlight. "But there's another option for me."

"With the priest, you mean?" Victor laughed. "Platonic love will grow old."

Kyle looked away, as if ashamed.

"Oh, I see. The priest has violated his vow. Hasn't he?"

"It was just once," Kyle stammered. "It'll never happen again."

"Of course not," Victor said with exaggerated conviction. "You'll both swear on the Bible to keep your bodies and hearts chaste."

Kyle glared at him. "Christ is with him. You can't touch him."

Victor settled back gleefully in his chair. He had been waiting for Kyle to introduce this subject. "I have a message for you to convey to your new chaste lover. His great mentor isn't what she seems. He believes that she's the messenger for his god. She's anything but that. She's an ambassador of the Dark Kingdom. She's using him to get to me. She wants him to tempt you away from me. So I won't make another vampire."

"You're lying."

"Look into my eyes, thrall. And see that I'm speaking the truth."

Kyle obeyed. And his own eyes widened in alarm. "Why doesn't she just kill me, if she's worried about that?"

"She can't. She doesn't have the power. You're mine, one way or another." Victor rolled back the sleeve of his shirt, and extended his arm to Kyle, tearing at the flesh with his teeth. "Go ahead. Take it."

Troubled, Kyle squeezed his eyes shut as though to resist, but he quickly abandoned the effort, getting up and kneeling before Victor's chair. As he drank, his eyelids fluttered and his eyes rolled back from sheer ecstasy.

When he finished, Victor took him by the chin and lifted his face. "Listen to your instincts. What's greater, your fear of me or your longing for me?"

Kyle's pain-filled gaze revealed the answer.

"Yes. You see that I have everything you want. You will face the priest, and tell him you want nothing more to do with him. And tell him if he wants confirmation of his mentor's true nature, he will find it in a mausoleum at St. Louis Cemetery."

10

I can't believe they've held up so long." Charles lay awake on the floor of Pete's room, staring at the glow-in-the dark stars fixed on the ceiling. Pete was on the bed next to him. They'd just switched off the light.

After the shameful episode with Kyle, he started spending the night at his parents' house, safe from temptation. Kyle could stay at his apartment for now, away from Victor, until they found another place for him. Charles sacked out in Pete's room because his own old room now held his mother's treadmill and big-screen TV, which she watched while she logged her predawn miles. He'd told his parents he needed a place to stay while his furnace was being worked on.

"I remember the day you put those stars up there," Charles continued. "You must have been in the fifth grade."

"Sixth," Pete said. "The year I bought my first telescope. I saved my paper-route money for a whole year to pay for it."

Charles chuckled. "I remember. You worked your butt off, pedaling that bike." Pete had always been a worker—delivering the *Times-Picayune* in grade school, flipping burgers in high school. "The job at McDonald's paid for the second telescope. Didn't it? I remembered how pissed Mom was that you wanted to spend your money on that instead of a tux for junior prom."

Pete laughed. "She wanted me to take Amy Duvier."

"The girl who just got her braces taken off. I remember. She had a crush on you."

"Kept showing up at the front door with brownies. She wasn't bad," Pete reflected. "I might have taken her if it wasn't for the telescope." After a long pause, his tone turned serious. "What happened, Charles? Between you and Kyle."

Charles had been waiting for the question. Pete hadn't probed Charles for three nights, patiently waiting for him to open up. But Charles's shame had run too deep to speak, and Pete knew his brother needed prodding now. Charles finally confessed quietly, "I broke my vow of celibacy, Pete."

"You made love with Kyle?"

"We had sex," Charles blurted, defensively, not wanting what happened to be more than lust. Lust meant he could simply ask God's forgiveness and put that night behind him—eventually.

"It wasn't just sex if you love him, Charles. You told me you thought you did love him. You do. You know it now, don't you?"

Pain rose in Charles's chest. It choked him, and he couldn't respond.

Pete reached down and touched his shoulder. "Love is good, Charles. It doesn't matter who you love. Does he love you?"

"I don't know. And it's killing me, Pete." Despite himself, Charles longed to know that Kyle loved him. Even though they could never have a future together. Kyle was trapped in a nightmare existence. And Charles had promised God to be celibate.

"If he does love you, maybe God is telling you something."

"Jesus, Pete," Charles snapped. "You know what he is! You know the monster who made him."

"Then save him!" Pete said, unyielding. He gripped Charles's shoulder. "You've gotta save him."

"How do I do that?" Charles said. "Do you have a textbook explaining how to free a thrall from his vampire host?"

Pete appeared to ponder the question. "Why can't you continue the way you have been?" he finally said.

Charles had told Pete about Kyle's method of survival.

"Even if we did, Victor would still call all the shots. Kyle's life depends on him. And Kyle lives in a state of limbo. It might as well be hell."

"But it's not hell." Pete spoke with amazing confidence. "Not if you love him."

In the morning, Charles left his Vespa at his parents' house and set out for his apartment by foot. The day was beautiful and he wanted to walk. In the mild air, a breeze stirred the sweet odor of some blooming flower. If only he were a different person, not an ordained man of God, he could relish the pleasurable sensation rushing through him in the sunlight—the feeling of being in love. He'd never experienced this lightness, this crazy, silly joy. The feeling was so wonderful, it seemed impossible that it could be "disordered," as the Church taught. But the Church had to be right, didn't it? The Church was instituted by Christ himself. Charles could never, never act on this feeling again. He had to make this clear to Kyle. But it was the last thing he wanted to do. So he circled the block when he got to his building without going in—to postpone this announcement. Or was he simply afraid that he'd give in to his passion once more?

When he finally worked up the courage to open the gate to his building and enter the courtyard, he looked up and saw Kyle gazing down at him from the gallery. He wore a white T-shirt and jeans. He seemed to be waiting for him.

"I need to grab some clothes," he called up. He couldn't just yell out the real reason for coming.

But Kyle seemed to see through the excuse. He nodded doubtfully.

Charles climbed the stairs, passed Kyle, and entered his apartment. He went to the bedroom, where he stuffed underwear, socks, and a sweater into a canvas bag. The bed wasn't made yet. And the impression of Kyle's head was still on a pillow. The room smelled of Kyle—his deodorant or soap. On the dresser stood a crucifix that evidently belonged to Kyle. Charles picked it up and was examining the carved corpus when Kyle walked in.

"I guess the lore about crucifixes and vampires isn't true?" Charles said. "Since Victor lets you have one."

"It's not true. But you're wrong about Victor. He won't let me have one around. He says he's got no patience with delusions about criminal executions in a Roman province. I know it's a painful reminder of Joshu's death. I keep this one hidden." He hesitated. "You don't have to do this, you know. It's your apartment. I can leave."

"Where would you go?" Charles said.

"To a hotel." Kyle's gray eyes were sad.

"A hotel costs money. You don't have any." Charles longed to hold him.

Kyle nodded, realizing Charles was right. "Then I could stay in the living room. I promise to leave you alone."

Charles shook his head. "I don't trust myself." He swallowed hard. "I love you. Do you love me?"

"It's useless," Kyle said, evasively, "whether I do or don't."

"But do you?" Charles insisted. He took a step toward Kyle.

Kyle opened his mouth to answer, but apparently thought better of it and pressed his lips together resolutely before speaking again. "There's something I have to tell you. You better sit down." He nodded at the bed.

Alarmed, Charles replaced the crucifix and sat down.

Kyle remained standing near the dresser. "It's about the therapist you're seeing."

"Dr. Beauchamp?"

"She's not who she says she is. She's not really a therapist, let alone a religious therapist. God, that's the last thing she is."

"What do you mean?" Charles had told Kyle about Beauchamp, about the plethysmograph treatment, about Beauchamp's dedication to the Church. How could Kyle question her credentials?

"Her name is Tiresia. She's the one who transformed Victor into what he is."

"What are you saying?" Charles said, mystified. "That she made him a vampire? That was two thousand years ago."

"Yes. She's the one. Victor recognized her. She's here to make him go back with her to the Dark Kingdom."

As Kyle went on to explain, Charles remembered the encounter with Victor outside of Dr. Beauchamp's door. So this is what Victor had meant about Dr. Beauchamp's power. But Charles couldn't believe it. It was all too much.

"He's lying!" Charles blurted.

"Why should he?"

"Pure malice. Why else?"

Kyle's stared solemnly at him.

"You believe him." A sense of dread rose in Charles.

"Your power against Victor comes from her. Not from Christ. She's been using you to distract me from Victor. If I fell in love with you, I would never consent to be what he is. And she's protected you from him."

Stunned, Charles looked past Kyle at the crucifix.

"It's been Tiresia, Charles, not Christ. I'm telling you the truth."

"I can't believe it!" Determined to prove Kyle wrong, Charles got up and headed for the front door.

"Where are you going?" Kyle called after him.

Charles didn't answer. He ran down the stairs and across the courtyard.

"You won't find her!" Kyle yelled down from the balcony.

Charles paid no attention to Kyle's warning. He had to let Beauchamp reassure him. He had to hear her laughing at this wild story. Kyle couldn't be right. Victor had lied to him. He exited through the gate and hustled down Dumaine and up St. Ann all the way to Rampart. The blue shutters of Dr. Beauchamp's house were closed. The nearby buildings, houses and small businesses, showed no signs of activity either. Here and there, up and down the street, was a stray pedestrian or two. Some were occupants of the Quarter, on their way to work. A few tourists in ball caps and T-shirts inspected the storefronts. Standing on Beauchamp's iron stoop, Charles rang the doorbell, and then pounded the door. Beauchamp didn't answer. He moved down to the side of the house, to try the back door, but the little gate between Beauchamp's building and the house next door was locked.

"Dr. Beauchamp!" he yelled, his heart racing now.

When Beauchamp did not respond, he crossed Rampart and ran to St. Louis Cemetery, where according to Kyle, Beauchamp could be found. As he passed through the open gate, the bright sky suddenly darkened. A sea of clouds seemed to appear from nowhere, and the breeze now gusted into wind. He wound through the mausoleums to a central edifice that Kyle had described to him. It resembled a miniature temple, with columns all around. He tried the gate of the mausoleum and found it unlocked. As he swung open the door, he was surprised to see a sarcophagus against the wall, visible in the faint, gray light. On the lid was the effigy of a bishop in a flowing robe and miter. But the face beneath the miter was not what he expected to see, the face of a stoic patriarch. Instead, it belonged to a woman, beautiful and proud, her eyes wide open. He hesitated, afraid for a moment. But his determination overcame his fear. He dropped to his knees and shoved the stone lid with all his might, pushing it from the casket.

Dr. Beauchamp's sleeping face greeted him. He recoiled. In this moment of hesitation, the door slammed shut behind him, and of its own accord the stone cover slid back in place.

Charles shot to his feet in alarm.

"You're a prisoner now," a disembodied voice pronounced in the low, feminine tone that he recognized as Beauchamp's. "See what existence awaits you in the tomb."

Charles went to the door and tried the latch. It was locked. He pounded the door and called out for help.

"It's useless," she said. "Rest with the dead now."

Charles continued to pound the door and cry out. But no one came to the rescue. There was a good chance that he was the only visitor in the cemetery. He finally turned and faced the dark tomb, waiting for his eyes to adjust. But not a crack of light traced the darkness. He probed the walls for a loose stone, but found none. He began to feel that the tight, black space was closing in on him. Starting to panic, he tried to slow his breathing, illogically afraid that he might deplete the air in the tomb.

To keep his head, he sank to his knees and began to pray aloud. "Hail Mary, full of grace, the Lord is with Thee." When he reached the final words of the Ave—pray for us sinners, now and at the hour of our death—Beauchamp's deep-throated laughter echoed through the vault.

Suddenly, of its own accord, the lid of the sarcophagus slid aside, exposing her face, which glowed weirdly as though she wore the luminescent white mask of a skull. He shrank back against the door and stayed there staring at the ghastly face, once again calling for help. But no one came. He felt exhausted, defeated. He sank to the floor, staring at the sarcophagus.

For a horrible hour he sat there staring at the face, unable to move, bracing himself for whatever encounter lay ahead. The air was cool, and after shivering for an hour, he had to relieve himself. Finally, summoning defiance, he got up and urinated in the corner. Immediately, the liquid steamed in his face, and the whole tomb heated like an oven.

"Stop!" he shouted.

But the tomb grew hotter and hotter. Desperate, he pounded on the door. Sweat ran down his back and sides. He mopped his face with his shirt. Then suddenly the temperature plunged. Within seconds he was freezing. He rubbed his damp arms and pounded his feet on the stone floor. Shuddering, he fell on the sarcophagus.

"Please!" he said. "Please."

Sinking to the floor, he hugged himself, and trembling, lost consciousness.

When he opened his eyes again, the tomb was aglow. He raised his head to see a torch mounted to the wall. The woman he had known as Dr. Beauchamp stared down at him from a throne. She wore a shimmering gold robe. Her head was wrapped in a gold turban. Her lips were as red as two oozing wounds.

"Jesus!" Charles got to his feet and drew back.

Her beauty was as shocking to him as her supernatural state.

Her eyes were black as onyx, the pupils indistinguishable from the irises. Her heavy eyelids glittered with gold. Gold loops hung from her earlobes.

"So, how do you like the truth?" she said.

"I don't." He strained away from her frightening beauty and power.

"You'd rather continue in the lie."

"I don't know what lie you're talking about."

"The lie that you are cured. You're as diseased as ever, aren't you?"

Charles truly did feel diseased now, physically and emotionally. And he felt abandoned by God. "So the joke's on me. My nature's the same. Always will be."

Tiresia dismissed his remark with a wave of her long, tapered fingers, their nails as red as her lips. "What difference does it make *how* you save him? Isn't that what you want? It's the—loving thing, isn't it?" She seemed to search for the word *loving* as though it came from a language foreign to her.

Charles was too overwhelmed to respond.

"You do want to save him, don't you?"

"Yes," Charles finally blurted, hating her. "From you!"

"So do it," Tiresia said with a shrug.

"Just how do I do that?" Charles said sarcastically, glancing around the tomb that imprisoned him.

"It is not an easy thing to admit, for one with my nature, but I have no power to harm you or your new friend. Especially your new friend. He belongs to the one who transformed him. That's why I rely on you. Don't tell me you would abandon him simply to frustrate my wishes. Our goal is the same. Does it matter if our motives are not?"

"Hell yes," Charles retorted. "Why should I trust you?"

"Better me than an impotent being from Heaven."

"That's blasphemy!"

Tiresia smiled. "Such piety! I hope you'll forgive me," she added ironically. "I certainly have no reason to blaspheme against your god. Heaven is no threat to me, and I bear no animosity to any of its inhabitants."

A sick feeling welled up in the pit of Charles's stomach. "You're saying Heaven really has no power over you. It's just one more supernatural place."

"That is precisely what I am saying."

"No." Charles shook his head. "I can't believe that."

Tiresia eyed him smugly. "You *won't* believe it. Be that as it may, you have owed your power to the Dark Kingdom. Why not exploit it? Carry on with your new friend with impunity. You enjoy his charms, and he enjoys your protection. And you do want to save him from his host?"

Charles felt no need to respond, and Tiresia knew it. Of course he wanted to save Kyle.

"Everyone wins. Everyone but Victor. And with him it's all a matter of pride. He has no need of this thrall. He can create another if he would like."

"But not another like Kyle. Not another who might consent to be a vampire—and turn Victor into a vampire maker. That's your only concern."

"Yes. And you should share my concern. Do you want to unleash another vampire in your precious world? The first of many? Do you want Victor to become a vampire maker? Whether you like it or not, we are on the same side."

The thought sickened Charles, but he knew she was right. "But I can't save Kyle. Can I? I can't save his soul."

Tiresia lifted her chin and fanned her face with her hand.

"This conversation is becoming tiresome. I have no desire to talk about such a ridiculous matter."

"Tell me! Can Kyle find salvation?"

"Your words make no sense to me. Salvation? From what? For what?"

"From evil. For everlasting life."

Tiresia laughed. "There are many kinds of everlasting life."

"Only one that Kyle and I care about."

Tiresia cast him a coy, sidelong glance. "How can you be so sure? The thrall is in love with his master. Give him time, and he will come to his senses. After all, he's very, very young in his kind of existence. He won't be able to resist Victor forever. Everything about his nature fights that resistance."

The words unsettled Charles. He knew how much Kyle struggled against his temptations.

"But why are we even discussing this?" Tiresia placidly raised her palms. "As I have said. Your reasons are irrelevant to me, as mine must be to you. You would not send him back to Victor, would you?"

"So Kyle was right," Charles said defeatedly. "You were the one who protected me from Victor. Not Christ."

"The powers of the Dark Kingdom protected you. Just as they will continue to do—not because they feel any affection for you, but because Victor must not succeed."

"What about the visions I had?"

"I know nothing about visions," Tiresia said, impatiently.

"The visions of Christ! The visions that cured me."

"Cured you of your shameful sensuality?" Tiresia laughed. "The powers did that, and they brought you to me when you sought a guide to keep yourself from lapsing back into your perverse nature."

Charles was confused. If Christ had not appeared to cure him, then why had he appeared?

Tiresia scrutinized him to determine what he was thinking. "If all you seek is freedom from your nature, the powers could assist you once again."

Charles exploded. "I don't want your benefits! I don't want to be cured by the devil. I'd rather be sick."

"You speak rashly now. You'll reconsider when your head clears."

"No." Charles got up and boldly approached the throne, his eyes now level with Tiresia's.

Tiresia glared at him, and he felt some kind of invisible force like a glass wall pushing against him. He couldn't take another step.

"Don't try my patience," the seeress said, raising her hand menacingly.

Charles took a step back.

Satisfied, Tiresia lowered her hand and reflected a moment. "You refuse our assistance. Very well. You will serve us yet."

The light suddenly vanished from the chamber. A wave of nausea passed through Charles's belly. He sank back against the wall. Gradually he recovered and felt for the door. The latch turned easily. When he pushed the door open, he beheld a cemetery bright with moonlight. He turned back to inspect the mausoleum, visible in the moon's rays. Tiresia and her throne had disappeared, and the floor where the sarchophagus lay was now bare.

That evening after Mass, he sank to his knees and prayed that what he had learned from Tiresia was false. That God and not evil powers had cured him. That if he renounced Kyle, his purity would be restored. *I'll do it, God. I will renounce him, no matter what happens to him. He's in with the Devil. He'll pull me into hell with him. Save me, Christ.*

After an hour on his knees, he was exhausted. He left the cathedral and went to his parents' house. His mother and father had nodded off in front of the television. Pete's room was empty. Charles panicked. He envisioned Victor feeding at Kyle's throat. He searched the house and then went to the backyard.

He found Pete there, gazing through his telescope. He felt relieved.

"Take a look at the moon," Pete said.

He moved aside, and Charles peered through the telescope at the bright, pock-marked orb. "It's beautiful." He turned to Pete, who now sat on a lawn chair. He considered telling his brother about the encounter with Tiresia. But he did not want to relieve the horror—and the pain—of it. But the pain rose in him nonetheless. "I thought I was cured, Pete. I thought Christ had cured me. I was wrong."

"Cured you?" Pete looked at him, perplexed for a moment. Then he understood. "You mean, you thought Christ cured you of being gay." He shook his head. "That's pretty lame, Charles. I told you, you are who you are. God made you that way."

Charles's first impulse was to object. But what if Pete was right? "You really believe that?"

"Hell yes!" Pete squeezed Charles's arm.

Charles shook his head. "You're not just saying that because I'm your brother?"

"I'm saying it because it's true. Come on, Charles, we don't live in the Middle Ages. We've got the Kinsey Institute now. Modern psychology. There are gay governors, and bishops, and football players. Join the twenty-first century."

For a moment, Charles gave himself the luxury of imagining that Pete was right. Then he dismissed the thought, and turned his attention back to the moon.

For three days he prayed to resist his temptation. And he succeeded. When Kyle called him on his cell phone, Charles recognized the number and overcame his urge to answer. Then, the next evening, Kyle showed up at Mass. He looked pale in his gray sweater. When he came up to receive communion, Charles noticed circles under his eyes. Charles let his hand linger on Kyle's palm when he deposited the wafer there. After Mass, as Charles removed his vestments in the sacristy, he considered leaving through the back door in case Kyle was waiting for him. But he couldn't bring himself to do it. He went out into the church, hoping that Kyle was still there. And he was, quietly sitting in a front pew. Charles sat next to him, saying nothing until the elderly man lighting a votive candle near them genuflected and hobbled away. Then he held Kyle's hand.

"You don't look good," he said.

"I stopped feeding."

Charles stared at him, alarmed.

Kyle's eyes remained fixed on the altar. "It's the only way," he said. "Victor won't end my life. I can't take it myself, not without committing a mortal sin. But God can't hold this against me. He can't punish me for refusing to drink a ghoul's blood. Can he?" Kyle turned to Charles now, imploringly.

Charles desperately wanted Kyle to save himself the only way he could. But how could he send him to the darkness, the very darkness he himself had renounced?

"Victor was telling the truth about Tiresia, wasn't he?" Kyle continued.

"Yes."

"You saw her? The way she really is?"

Charles nodded solemnly. "She wants me to save you," he answered. "Ironic, isn't it? When someone so evil wants the same thing that God wants. And God does want it, Kyle!" Charles squeezed Kyle's hand.

Kyle pulled his hand away. "She doesn't want the same thing God wants. She doesn't care a damn about my soul."

"You can't do this!" Charles blurted. "Not even if you wanted to. You're programmed to feed for his sake."

"Maybe he's letting me go. He can will anything."

"No!" Charles couldn't believe it. "He wants power too much. He won't let you go. He has something planned."

"But if I resist, it'll show God I don't want this life. I'll be redeemed."

Charles suddenly hated God. "Is God really like that? Does he make us prove ourselves? I'm not so sure it's worth it."

"Never say that!" Kyle said, fire in his eyes. "What's your brief life compared to life in heaven? My kind of life is an eternity of hell."

Charles thought for a moment before making the declaration on his mind. "I'd do anything to free you. I'm in love with you." He gripped Kyle's hand and Kyle let him this time. "Please don't stop feeding!"

"When I feed, I'm his. Body and soul. Do you really want that?"

"I don't want you to die."

"Then you're being selfish." Kyle turned away.

"All right." Desperate, Charles conceded, despite himself. "If that's what you want. We'll wait it out together. Give God a chance."

They sat in silence a few moments before Kyle stood to leave. Charles wanted to hold him back. He wanted to embrace him. But he made himself stay behind as Kyle exited the church.

For the rest of the day, Charles kept himself occupied. He visited a homebound parishioner whose sight was failing, and he visited classrooms at Holy Rosary School, which had just reopened, to give catechism lessons. While he was telling the story of Adam and Eve in a third grade classroom, a little girl in a plaid uniform raised her hand and asked how the Devil got inside the snake in the Garden of Eden.

"Oh, the Devil's just clever, Renee," Charles answered. "But God keeps him in line. The Devil can't hurt you, because God is protecting you."

"But God made Adam and Eve leave the garden." The girl's short pigtails stuck straight out on either side of her head.

"He still loved them. It was just time for them to start a family."

"Did God send Hurricane Katrina?"

"No. Hurricanes just happen."

"But why didn't God stop it?"

Charles sighed and shrugged. "I don't know."

"He wanted to punish queers." The boy who yelled this was so blond that his eyebrows were nearly invisible.

"Who told you that?" Charles said.

"My pop. He said that New Orleans was like Sodom in the Bible that God burned down because of queers."

"Don't use that word, Max."

"My pop does."

"Your pop is a grown-up. I can't tell him what to do. But you need to mind me in school."

A mischievous glint suddenly appeared in Max's eyes. "Pop said he'd like to take his shotgun and clean the queers out of Bourbon Street."

"Then he'd be put in jail," Charles said matter-of-factly, and continued with his lesson.

That night he thrashed in bed, feeling desperate and confused. How could he let Kyle destroy himself? He wanted Kyle to live, no matter how unbearable the young man's bondage to Victor was. He loved Kyle so much he thought he might die himself if he didn't have him. Why did God permit this longing? Why had Christ not cured him of it, if He expected Charles to be faithful to his vows?

Finally Charles got up and went to the cathedral, desperate to pray. But when he tried, he found he couldn't. He couldn't find even a modicum of peace. For an hour, he stared at the sanctuary flame, frustrated and angry. At last he gave up. He needed a drink. He left the cathedral and walked to Bourbon Street, entering a bar he hadn't patronized since his college days. The doors were wide open. A music video flashed on a screen over the bar, the beat pounding all the way out to the street. It was three in morning, and just a few men stood at the bar. Charles ordered a bourbon and Coke, and perched on a chair by a cocktail table near an open door.

He'd finished half of his drink when a man of sixty or so in a Hawaiian shirt strolled over to the table. He had a mop of iron-colored hair and a brown, lined face, as though he'd just spent two weeks on the decks of a cruise ship, enjoying a vacation package for seniors. Judging from the paunch beneath his shirt, he'd enjoyed the buffets on the cruise. He was holding a plastic cup. Charles could smell beer on his breath.

"You look lonely over here," he said to Charles. "Mind if I join you? I'm Herb."

Charles nodded, indifferent, shaking the hand that Herb offered him. "Charles," he managed to say.

"Looks like things are starting to get back to normal in New Orleans. First time I've been here since the hurricane. I'm from Jackson." His Mississippi drawl was strong. "You from New Orleans?"

Charles nodded.

"You come out of the storm all right?"

"I guess." Charles watched the bartender show off a tattoo on his forearm to a man with a long braid down his back.

"Well, I'm sure as hell glad the Quarter held up. The rest of the city—I don't give a rat's ass about. No offense. But at Mardi Gras and in between, the Quarter is where I spend my time. Some pretty boys here. And I don't mean the hustler scum." He gestured with his drink to a scrawny boy with bleached hair sitting at the bar, elbows on the counter, gesturing with a cigarette at the bartender's tattoo.

"You know, a lot of people lost everything they had," Charles said, surly now.

Herb laughed. "Don't I know it. Saw plenty of their sorry asses in Jackson. The niggers didn't stay long 'round us. We don't have many bleeding hearts in my town."

Charles drained his drink and walked away without another word.

"Hey, Chuck! Where you off to?" Herb called after him, following him and grabbing his arm.

Charles yanked himself away. "Go to hell!"

"Well, Jesus H. Christ!"

Charles waved a middle finger at him and exited the bar.

He hit three more bars on Bourbon. By dawn, he was so drunk he could barely get to the bathroom on the second floor of a dark, noisy club with two go-go boys on the bar. As he stood at the urinal, wobbling, he felt a hand on his arm.

"Hey, sailor, steady as she goes."

He glanced over his shoulder and saw the man with the braid down his back, from the first bar he'd visited. His dark eyes and goatee were blurry, but Charles could see that he was handsome.

"Had too much," Charles said, zipping his fly and flushing.

"Who says?"

When Charles turned around, the man took hold of his shoulders. "Let me see." He examined Charles's face. "Naw, I think you're just fine." He patted Charles's chest. His hand traveled down to Charles's crotch, and he got closer. "Wanna go to my place?"

"Sure."

Charles followed him out of the bathroom and down the stairs, supporting himself on the handrail. They passed through the crowd around the bar and went out to the street.

"You okay?" the man said. "I'm up on St. Ann's."

"Great," Charles said perfunctorily, kissing him on the lips.

The man smiled. "I'm Jeff."

"Lead on, Jeff."

"What's your name?

"I don't have a name."

Jeff smiled and raised his hands. "Hey, whatever you want."

Jeff's apartment was above a bookstore on St. Ann's. They climbed the stairs and entered a living room cluttered with camera equipment. A library table in the corner was spread with photographs. Framed black and white shots of the flooded, devastated city covered one wall. In one shot, a young woman and two children sat on a flat section of the roof of a house, which barely cleared the brown water.

Charles studied the poignant photograph. The expression on the woman's face was more of exhaustion than desperation. One child lay with her head on the woman's lap, while the other child, a boy, pounded the roof with a stick.

"How did you take this?" Charles said, his head beginning to spin.

"Went out on a boat with a pal of mine. You want something to drink?" Jeff massaged Charles's back.

Charles shook his head.

Smiling mischievously, Jeff squatted and unbuttoned Charles's jeans and pulled down his briefs. His mouth groped for Charles's penis, his tongue warm as bathwater.

Charles squeezed his eyes shut to steady himself, resting his hands on Jeff's silky hair. Then he suddenly jerked away. "No," he muttered. "I gotta leave." He buttoned himself up and stumbled toward the door.

"Come on, man," Jeff called after him. "We don't have to do anything."

Charles didn't stop. He descended the stairs and headed for Dumaine, weaving on the sidewalk. He managed to make it home and up to his apartment.

"Kyle," he shouted as he stepped into the living room, still dark in the faint light of dawn. Without turning on a light, he felt his way to the bedroom. The door was open. He leaned against the door frame. "Kyle," he called. He groped toward the luminescent figure on the bed and climbed in next to it.

Suddenly he found his arms pinned back, and the glowing face that stared at him was not Kyle's. It was Victor's!

"They say that foes make excellent lovers," Victor said, his voice deep and soft.

"Jesus!" Charles struggled against Victor's hold, but he might as well have tried to heave a fallen oak from his body.

"Why resist?" Victor's mouth found Charles's throat.

Charles felt the sharp fangs and braced himself.

"You shouldn't worry about betraying my thrall. I've just enjoyed him and sent him away to give you a turn." Victor stretched his naked body over Charles.

Charles's head stopped spinning from the alcohol. His senses were suddenly keen. His body felt porous, waiting to drink in Victor. *He's a monster*, he said in his mind. *He attacked Pete. He's made Kyle's life a living hell.* But no matter how adamant his mental protests, they didn't diminish his euphoria. Was Victor's supernatural will bending his own mortal one? Or was his own perverse lust overwhelming him? Somehow, it felt like both. Victor and his own dark longings merged as he opened his mouth and spread his limbs like a sadistic martyr, while Victor stripped and conquered him. When they had both climaxed, Charles lay panting, blood sliding down his belly from the gashes Victor's fangs left in his flesh. As Victor lapped the liquid, he moaned and his eyes rolled back in his head.

The front door opened. Despite his alarm, Charles was too spent to get up from the bed. He lay prone and sweating, when Kyle flicked on the light. He stood in the doorway, his flesh pallid against his black pullover.

Victor laughed without turning his face from Charles's belly. "You see?" he said. "I told you there's no refuge from me. He'll succumb again, and so will you. So what's the use trying to cast off your nature?"

"I wanted salvation," Kyle said in a soft, defeated voice.

"You need to revise your idea of that."

"I'm sorry," Charles muttered, knowing that any show of shame was useless.

"He's right," Kyle said. "Why run? I'll be at home, Victor." He turned and left the room. The front door shut quietly behind him.

Victor grinned, tracing his fingers on Charles's chest. "Yes, he'll be at home."

Charles felt groggy. His inebriation, held in strange abeyance during his passion with Victor, suddenly descended on him again. He tried to focus his eyes as Victor dressed. He told himself he should get up and attack him. But he could summon no strength. His head was heavy as a rock, sinking deeper and deeper into a soft oblivion.

PART III

PARADISO

Nel ciel che più de la sua luce prende
fu' io, e vidi cose che ridire
né sa né può chi di là sù discende

*(I was in the heaven that most receives [God's] light
and I saw things which he that descends from it
has not the knowledge or the power to tell again)*

—Dante Alighieri

11

Dark as a cave, with the statuary and arches like rocky forma-
tions, the cathedral, Victor felt, belonged to him. As an act of
defiance, he had led his thrall to these sacred shadows for their
interview. The time for hesitation was over. He craved the power
awaiting him as a vampire maker, and the time was ripe for his
thrall to choose.

Under the dark vault, Victor leapt fifty feet to the organ loft at
the rear of the nave. Like a gargoyle, he perched on the rail, peering down at Kyle, who stared up at him from the aisle as though
he stood at the gates of the Inferno, awaiting his assigned circle
of Hell.

"*Lasicate ogni speranza voi ch'entrate!*" Victor's voice boomed
through the cavernous chamber. "Do you recognize the words?
Abandon all hope, ye who enter here! It's from Dante. Look
around, Kyle. This place holds all your delusions of another immortality. It's mocking you. It makes promises it can't keep. Not
for someone with your nature. So it's time to choose. Either live
under my thumb as you are, or join me in my existence—as an
equal. You should be very, very pleased with my largesse. I'm offering a share in my assigned territory on the earth."

"Why not just kill me, and find another candidate?" Kyle cried bitterly.

Victor laughed. "You don't want me to kill you. You're afraid of what awaits you on the other side. Of course, you shouldn't be. There's no hell for your kind. A thrall who no longer serves his purpose is sent to oblivion. And that you *should* fear."

Kyle stared up at him, desperation in his face. "Then tell me something. Do you . . . do you really love me?"

Victor found himself moved by the question. His heart cried yes, but he knew the argument that Kyle would make if he confessed the truth. *If you love me, it doesn't matter whether I'm a thrall or one of your kind.* So he restrained himself. "I love you as a thrall," he said. "But become like me, and my love will become something more. Surrender and find the immortality you've always longed for."

"I've never longed for what you have."

"Knowledge transforms, doesn't it? Now you have the knowledge of Prometheus. The secret of the gods. Their fire. Forget final repercussions. There are none. Be with me for the allotted period as a vampire. Then go to our own brand of heaven—if after two centuries you still crave a heaven of some kind."

"I don't have a choice."

"Wrong." Victor could see that Kyle was yielding, despite his objections. His own heart raced. He was excited at the prospect of a true marriage with Kyle. "You do have a choice. Everything is in your hands. I can't force your consent. Or I would."

Kyle stared up in silence. He turned to survey the nave, the high altar.

"Pray for guidance, if you want," Victor taunted.

"Do you really think I can take *his* place? That's all you want. But it won't work. It never has."

Victor glared down at Kyle, suddenly wanting to pounce on him. Whatever the truth about his obsession for Joshu, no one, least of all his thrall, should dare to throw it in his face. But he exerted his will to control himself. He could use the remark to his advantage. "Maybe I haven't found the right substitute," he said. "Give me this chance." As soon as he said the words, a sense of desperation welled in him. The words were truer than he'd intended.

"All right," Kyle said. "I consent. Do it now."

Victor peered at him doubtfully. "Do you mean it?"

"I believe you," Kyle explained, defeatedly. "If I don't consent, I'll never leave this limbo."

"No. You won't. I promise."

"Then do it!" Kyle screamed. "Do it, now!" He fell on his knees, his arms outstretched. The sound of his voice echoed in the empty nave.

"Not now," Victor said. The thrall's act of submission satisfied him as always, but his satisfaction now rested mostly in his triumph over Tiresia and the Dark Kingdom. Especially over Joshu. Exerting his power was always, in some strange way, an act of defiance against Joshu. But to conquer a priest was a most delicious act of revenge.

Victor sailed down from the loft and embraced Kyle passionately. Then they left the cathedral, quietly strolling back to the mansion. Victor savored his joy in the damp night air. Halfway home, he stopped and pulled Kyle to him, kissing his docile lips.

When they entered the mansion, Victor led Kyle by the hand up the dark stairs and into their bedroom. He stripped Kyle, then himself, and guided him to the bed. Kyle's flesh seemed especially malleable under Victor's rough touch, but the thrall received Victor's tongue, and fangs, and phallus with a sense of anticipation rather than with the fatalism that had colored his passion over the past four years. Could it be that Victor's slave truly thrilled to the new level of existence before him? That his will—in his act of acquiescence—had finally consented to the transformation Victor offered?

"Marvels await you," Victor whispered into Kyle's ear. Then he tugged at it playfully with his teeth. "But you must be prepared. The changes are enormous. Your strength, the acuteness of your senses, the ability to look into minds and to transport yourself with a thought, you have no idea of the power. Mortals overestimate their abilities. With you that will never be possible. Even when you exercise your powers, you'll hardly believe them. At first it will seem like a foreign being has possessed you, as though your flesh acts apart from your will. But it is your will. Your least conscious act of volition will yield immediate results."

"It scares me," Kyle whispered, stroking Victor's cheek.

"Your own power? Why should it?"

"Because your kind of power always dominates. It's deadly."

Victor chuckled. "You can dismiss that fear. Once you share my nature, your sympathies will correct themselves. Do you regret your power to smash an insect? Of course not."

"And what kind of a conscience does a vampire have? Or does he have one at all?"

"I think you'll be relieved to lose your conscience."

"Then I really will lose it?"

"I don't have much patience for discussion of moral character." Victor slapped Kyle's taut belly. "What's the point? But I will remind you that I have loved. Usually despite myself."

"You mean affection."

"Is there another kind of love?"

"There's sacrificial love."

"I'm tired of this." Victor sat up, suddenly irritated. "I'm going out to feed."

"Wait." Kyle grabbed his arm. "I'm ready for it. I'm ready to throw caution to the wind."

Kyle had his attention now. Victor settled back on the bed.

Kyle sat up against the headboard. He drew his knees up and clasped his hands around them. "I'm tired of living half a life. That's what I'm saying. My old life is gone. It won't come back. The eternity I imagined isn't there anymore. Not for me, at least. This will be a new start. You and me together like gods. We can love each other. That's what I'm saying. We can put our lives on the line for each other. Sacrificial love. Don't say it!" Kyle held up his hand when Victor smiled. "You don't think it's in your nature. But it is. And even if it isn't, I don't care. That's how I want to live. That kind of love will redeem me."

Victor touched Kyle's stubbled cheek. "We'll see what you want after your transformation. You don't know yet what it's like to have the kind of power I have. You may not be so ready to lay down your life. I promise you, I never will. Have no delusions."

"I knew you'd say that. You have to."

"Yes. And it's true. I feel no compulsions to confess anything to you. You know it's true."

"You really think there's no goodness in you? Why do you think you keep looking for him?"

Victor bristled. He leveled his gaze at Kyle. "This is a subject that you will not broach. Not ever. Not as my thrall, certainly. Not even as a vampire."

"Why be ashamed of it? It's why I love you."

"Then keep it to yourself."

The next day, Victor easily secured another coffin for the mausoleum by breaking into a mortuary abandoned after the hurricane. With Kyle's help, he transported the coffin to the cemetery in the dark of night with a pickup truck he stole for the occasion. The lock on the cemetery gate broke easily under his strength, and they carried the coffin to Victor's mausoleum and laid it on the floor next to Victor's.

"I should climb into it," Kyle said. "To see what if feels like."

Victor disliked the idea. "What if you hate it? Don't be foolish. There's a world of difference between entering a coffin now and entering it when you have risen from it again and again—when the sight of it is a comfort. But how can you see it in such light now? You associate it with death. The death of people you have known and loved."

"But I should be prepared."

"Were you prepared for the first man you wanted? You don't need preparation for what is primal."

"I won't change my mind," Kyle said resolutely.

"That's all I want to know." Victor kissed him softly on the mouth.

When sunset arrived again, Victor spent the evening examining his financial records. He had amassed an enormous fortune over the centuries—investing all that he had stolen from his victims the world over. He wanted to protect all access to the documents from Kyle. Equal or not, soulmate or not, who knew what effect Kyle's new powers would have on his character? Power, like money, can corrupt the soul. Granted, corrupt souls were far more intriguing than pious ones, but he was not a fool. His wealth he would gladly share with his vampire lover, but never the access to it.

After Kyle drifted off to sleep in the early hours of the morning, Victor set out for the French Quarter to feed. But as he lifted into the night, a storm broke loose. The sudden winds bent the limbs of trees. Lightning flashed and rain pelted him. Then *her* voice sounded through the night sky. The voice of Tiresia. He felt himself changing course, in the direction of the tombs of St. Louis Cemetery, as though the winds themselves drove him there. When he reached the city of the dead, he lighted in the center of the sepulchers. Lightning flashed on the white tombs. The rain beat his face, but he lifted it to the storm and waited for her.

She appeared before him, suspended above the ground, her dreadlocks flying about her face like a dark aureole in frenzy. Her shuddering white robe cast a deathly light on her brown features. She extended her arms as if to embrace the storm, of her own creation, Victor knew. Then she lowered them, and the tempest subsided. She floated down, seated on a high throne that came from nowhere. In the new silence, the trees still dripping, she admired him. Victor returned her admiration.

"Tell me," she finally said, "of your existence following my departure to the Dark Kingdom."

"Why repeat what you already know?"

"The inhabitants of the Dark Kingdom do enjoy a certain omniscience, but why should we bother ourselves with the dull lives of vampires on earth?"

"Indeed. Why bother yourself now?"

"Because I transformed you. You are my creation. I have a genuine affection for you, as hard as that is for you to believe."

"I'm no one's creation. You merely provided a means to escape the authorities."

Tiresia cocked her head and smiled wickedly. "And why did they pursue you? Who inspired your campaign of violence?"

Victor wanted to choke her for alluding to Joshu. Even an allusion from someone like her was an insult.

"Ah, I see I have offended you."

"I don't like rhetorical questions. I'm not your student. If you have something to say, then say it."

"Very well." Tiresia smiled and clasped her hands on her lap. "What I wish to convey is the affection that led me to offer you a new existence. Of course, I wanted the Dark Kingdom and I needed to replace myself—and you should learn something from that deep desire of one so powerful on the earth, one who would gladly surrender this filthy, gloomy realm for eternal sunlight. But motives can be mixed. You stole my heart because your cruelty belied your vulnerability to love. Your transformation would allow you to pursue love." Tiresia tilted her head. "I see you doubt me. That's your nature, too, so I don't fault you. But please, tell me of your existence as a vampire. Have you found satisfaction?"

A chair suddenly appeared, and Tiresia motioned to it. Victor seated himself, deciding to humor her in order to discover her intentions for bringing him there. So he prosaically summarized his history. "I wandered from Rome to Asia. I wanted to see the world. When I returned, the Barbarians had begun to sack the city. I left the city and traveled to a monastery in Egypt, then to monasteries in North Africa. When monks came to Europe, I returned and used them for my shelter and my vengeance. That's the long and short of it."

"Vengeance, you said. Vengeance on *his* God."

"And on him."

"But also to pursue him. And to allow him to pursue you?"

"Yes." Victor had no reason to lie.

"But you have abandoned your pursuit. You no longer pose as a monk."

"It no longer amuses me."

"You sell yourself short. You hate to admit noble motives."

"I have never been accused of such a thing."

Tiresia dismissed the comment with a wave of her hand and leaned forward on her throne. "Listen to me, Victor. Your journey here has ended. For two millennia you have taunted him and pursued him. You have ruled your territory of the earth. Now to better things."

"I agree."

"You are deluded," she said, becoming impatient. "You cannot continue as a vampire maker."

"I already have. I don't believe the Dark Kingdom can intervene."

"We can. But it is tiresome to do so. Now listen to me. Take your rightful place, and we will grant you governing power there. We have our own hierarchy. You will be made Procurator."

"Procurator of what?" Victor challenged. "Who pays obeisance to me? Who can I torture if I choose? I don't believe you."

Angry now, Tiresia leveled her gaze at him. "Decisions must be made in the Dark Kingdom. The authorities there have sent me here. Authorities must enforce the cosmic order. You will move from an insignificant sphere on earth to a cosmic sphere."

"You think I'll find law enforcement attractive, especially of laws that I had no hand in issuing?"

"But you will have a hand. Take my word. The kind of power I offer you is beyond your comprehension. It is power not only in our own sphere, but in others."

Now Tiresia had his attention. "Which spheres?"

"His."

The thought of it rendered him speechless. But he quickly

recovered himself. "I don't believe you. I could never have control over Joshu's sphere of eternity."

"Control may not be the correct word. But for your purposes, you will have all the power you could desire. Access to him. Isn't that what you want?"

Unconvinced, Victor stared at her. The sky had cleared, and a bright moon cast its rays on her face and snowy robe.

"Let me demonstrate." Tiresia raised her finger toward the moon. The orange sphere vanished.

Victor felt himself falling into the darkness. Then suddenly the day rose around him, and before him a body of water reached to the horizon. It lapped too calmly against the shore for it to be the ocean. Then he recognized the Sea of Galilee. His heart raced with expectation, and the one he linked to this view came walking along the shore toward him in a flowing tunic. Joshu's olive face was browned by the sun, as were his arms. His coarse chestnut hair gleamed with strands bleached to gold. His face belonged to the twenty-year-old youth that Victor had first encountered on the cliffs above Jerusalem. Seeing him there felt completely reasonable. All the centuries that had intervened between this scene and the present moment disappeared. The scene and the months leading to it had become the present moment for Victor. He had no consciousness of another time or existence.

"I brought bread and cheese." Joshu smiled, raising a bag made of sheepskin. "Where did you get the wine?" He nodded to a clay cask in Victor's hand.

"I gave a fisherman a gold denarius for it." Victor remembered the exchange quite clearly. The man had smelled of fish. And when he had smiled at the coin, he exposed rotten teeth.

"Let's sit here," Joshu said.

They sat on the sand, cross-legged. Joshu passed the bread

and cheese. They shared the cask. They talked little, perfectly comfortable in their silent company, their eyes moving from the placid water, where two fishing boats bobbed in the distance, to each other. This was their daily ritual, in Victor's mind.

"You're covered with dust," Joshu said, his mouth full of bread.

Victor noticed his own body for the first time. His muscular arms were covered with fine powder, and his sandaled feet were muddy. "The masons were mixing sand. They're finishing the courtyard today. It won't be long."

"My family will disown me, you know. They'll have no choice."

Victor waved a fly from Joshu's face. "I'll be all the family you need."

Their honeymoon had never waned. Victor had never felt so content. There was nothing more he could ever want. Joshu was everything. He only vaguely remembered his own occupation as an officer. His commission by the empire was fulfilled. His father had given him acres of vineyards, and he'd made his own wealth. The mansion in Caesarea Philippi, their new home, was nearly complete.

When they finished eating, they stripped off their tunics and jumped into the water. They swam away from the shore to deeper water and floated on their backs. The sun beat on their wet skin, and they both closed their eyes to enjoy the warmth. When Victor opened his eyes, Joshu was nowhere to be seen. Victor paddled in the water, scanning the area casually at first and then in a panic, finally plunging in and feeling about in the opaqueness for Joshu. When he broke through the surface, Joshu was there, smiling mischievously.

"Very funny," he said, perturbed.

"Don't you know I can walk on water?" Joshu said.

"I'll keep that in mind."

"Come on, I'll race you back to shore!" Joshu swam away, his muscular arms cutting through the water.

Victor pursued him, determined to win. He passed him midway to shore and raced on. But when he arrived at shallow water and stood, Joshu waved to him from shore, his wet body shining in the sunlight.

"Conjuring!" Victor said, approaching Joshu.

"That's a Roman name for it," Joshu answered.

"What's the Jew's name for it?"

"Superiority." Joshu laughed.

They both stretched out on the sand, Joshu laying his leg across Victor's. Victor reached for Joshu's hand and kissed it.

"Do you know what I want?" Joshu said. "I want to lie here forever next to you."

"It suits me." Victor closed his eyes, still clinging to Joshu's hand.

All of a sudden a cold current passed over his body. He opened his eyes and found himself in complete darkness. His hand was empty. He groped in the darkness for Joshu, but he had disappeared.

"Joshu!" He sprang to his feet and gazed toward the invisible water.

Lightning flashed. The jagged light coalesced into a disk. Directly in front of him, Tiresia, once again ensconced on a throne, glowed in the moon's rays.

"You wished the encounter to continue?" she said. "Imagine your power to make it happen at will. However long, whatever setting, whatever conversation your heart most desires between you and him."

"Illusions!" Victor said, his soul suddenly empty.

"Since when do immortal beings make such a distinction?

What isn't an illusion? And while the illusion lasts, it is a reality. You know how you felt with him now. Don't tell me the experience was not satisfying."

"Only until I awoke."

"We always awaken. The hope comes in knowing that dreams are at our disposal. Think of it, Victor." Tiresia stared intently at him. "You alone control the encounter—its length, its intensity, its details. You will have no awareness of its ephemeral quality. While you live in the world you create, it will be the only world possible in your understanding. Why quibble over technicalities? All that you have ever wanted from him, you will have."

Victor pondered the offer. All that he had ever wanted from Joshu? Over the centuries, the millennia, had he not imagined episode after episode of their life together? Could this be the answer to all of his desires? He scrutinized Tiresia's beautiful eyes for the truth.

"I see what you are thinking," she said. "I would not deceive the child of my creation."

"My mother?" Victor laughed. "Your moans of pleasure didn't sound like those of a mother."

"Of course, I'm speaking metaphorically," Tiresia snapped. "Call me what you will. You must believe that I would not deceive you."

"Must I?" Victor stood and made as if to leave.

"You want power!" Tiresia cried, with desperation. "Here is your opportunity. Take it, Victor."

Victor turned back to her. "Real power, it appears, lies in making another like me. What else would bring the likes of you here?"

"You're deceived. Any power you acquire in making another vampire will have its penalty. You have compared yourself to

Prometheus. Do you forget that eagles pecked at his liver when he was chained to the mountainside? Heed me. You will repent your creation. He will eat you alive."

"My thrall?" Victor laughed. "He's a boy. He's under my hand. He'd jump into hell if I told him to."

"Take what I offer, Victor! Not to submit, but to control the one who has eluded you all of these centuries. Consider it!"

Victor smiled at her clear frustration. He approached her, lifted her hand, cool as porcelain, and kissed it. "I thought I'd never see you again. Not in this world. I never will again, will I?"

Tiresia stared at him without answering.

"In Rome, all those centuries ago, why did you transform me without making me promise to join you in the Dark Kingdom?"

Tiresia pulled her hand away. "I didn't want you."

Victor laughed. "Impossible!"

Glaring, Tiresia faded into the night, stirring a fierce wind in her wake.

Victor peered into the darkness. The moment had come. His fangs descended in expectation. He lifted into the night, lighting finally on the portico of his mansion. He entered through the front door. In the parlor, a candelabrum glowed on the piano and a fire crackled in the hearth, its warmth cutting through the damp night air. There was movement on the stairs. Victor turned to see Kyle descending in a silk robe. He carried a glass of wine. Clearly not his first, by the look of his drunken gaze. He offered a crooked smile to Victor, and stumbled on the last step. Victor approached him and steadied him.

For a moment, Victor hesitated. Tiresia's offer was attractive. To summon Joshu when and where he liked, to lose himself in bliss with him—even temporarily—had magnificent appeal. Victor might even punish Joshu for the pain the man caused, punish before wiping clean the slate, not in pious forgiveness, but because once his anger was satisfied he could better enjoy their love. And yet, before him, in this soft-eyed boy, stood the possibility of real power, not simply power over dreams. His thrall offered yet another step toward an earthly kingdom of vampires, ruled by Victor the Vampire Maker. He lusted for such power, power not condescendingly bequeathed to him but wrested by him from cosmic forces. Tiresia's proposal had only heightened the lust. It required immediate satisfaction.

"Are you ready?" Victor said, clutching Kyle's arm.

"To be like you." Kyle nodded, his eyes heavy-lidded.

Victor snatched the glass from Kyle's hand and flung it to the floor. Wine from the broken glass spattered the wall. Victor untied the belt of Kyle's robe and slipped it from his shoulders, dropping it to the floor. In the candlelight, Kyle's strong body seemed smooth as soap, white and softly glowing. Victor stripped off his own shirt and drew Kyle's face to his breast.

"Drink!" he said.

Like an infant, Kyle found Victor's nipple, and he suckled.

An orgasmic sensation rose in Victor that lasted as long as Kyle drank. He gasped for air, his chest heaving. With his legs in danger of folding beneath him, he steadied himself against the newel post of the staircase. He stroked Kyle's smooth white back.

Spasms rippled through Kyle's body. He jerked away from Victor, clutching his throat, as if he were choking. He crumbled to the floor, still writhing. Suddenly the spasms ceased. He lay still as a corpse, and Victor knew Kyle had indeed lost his mortal life. Victor waited. Finally Kyle moaned. He opened his eyes, and raised them to Victor. Like a marionette controlled by invisible strings, his body rose in the air before settling again, his feet now planted firmly on the floor.

He was in control of himself now. His naked, athletic form was sturdy as a marble statue. His eyes shone like red lasers. He smiled wickedly.

"Now I know," he said, his voice strong. "Every moment of your life flashed through my mind. When you were a little boy, wrestling your brother Justin, the moment Tiresia transformed you into a vampire, your feedings over the centuries. I know you now, Victor. And you don't scare me. Because now I share your nature."

Victor saw Kyle in a new light now. He was no longer a parasitical thrall. He was strong. An equal. A true opponent. A true lover. Victor reached for Kyle to pull him close, but Kyle remained fixed in place. Still grinning, Kyle pulled Victor to him, opening his mouth to reveal his new fangs and kissing Victor hungrily. They made love on the floor, wrestling to gain superiority, to be the one who mounted and impaled and thrust. First Victor succeeded. Then Kyle. But Victor had the final triumph, exploding inside Kyle, with Kyle's lustful, bold gaze boring into him.

They dressed and went out into the night. The energy of Kyle's step and the young man's keen observation of the dark street told Victor that their unspoken task invigorated his new equal as much as it did him.

It wasn't long before their prey made its appearance. Down the sidewalk toward them from St. Charles Street walked a young man in a suit, carrying a briefcase. He seemed to hesitate at the sight of two strangers in the darkness. Then he reached inside the pocket of his coat and continued toward them.

As they approached him, Kyle lunged at man, knocking him off his feet. A shot went off. Kyle stared up at Victor, his eyes filled with pain. The man had fired a gun, and the bullet had wounded Kyle.

"It will heal in an instant," Victor assured him. Then Victor fell on the confused man, pinning back his arms and plunging fangs into his throat.

The man struggled only a moment before his body went limp. By then, Kyle had recovered. He examined the flesh beneath his shirt and looked surprised at finding no wound, though blood stained his hand. He knelt over the victim. Victor moved aside to let Kyle feed from the spot where he had been drinking. But Kyle shook his head. He plunged his fangs into a new place on the victim's throat and drank.

"Not too much!" Victor said. "Listen to the heartbeat. You'll know how far you can go."

He had already explained to Kyle the danger of drinking from a corpse. Even had he not, Kyle's own instincts would warn him to withdraw. However, new vampires did not always trust their instincts.

When Kyle raised his bloody mouth, he stared a moment into the face of his victim and then lifted the man's head.

"What are you doing?" Victor said.

"What do you think?" His eyes gleamed with cruel delight.

"There's no need to kill him. He can survive with this much loss of blood."

"But I want to." Without waiting for another objection, he quickly twisted the man's head until the spine snapped.

Then he did something that Victor had never seen in all of his life as a nocturnal predator—his vampire equal lifted his head to the night, bared his fangs, and howled like a wolf.

12

Ask and you shall receive. Seek and you shall find. Knock and the door shall be opened to you." Raising his eyes to the congregation before him, Charles paused after pronouncing the scriptural text on the pulpit. *It's all a lie*, he was thinking. *I asked to be made good and whole, and Christ ignored me. Worse yet, he let the powers of evil cure me—for their own purposes. And now I'm lost. I love a demon.*

Distracted and depressed, he went through the appropriate motions for the rest of the Mass. Afterward, he stood in the vestibule, shaking hands of departing parishioners.

"You all right, Father?" a petite African American woman with large green eyes said as she clasped his hand.

Charles nodded perfunctorily.

"We're so thankful you were assigned to the cathedral. You've given us the strength we need at a time like this, with the city still a mess."

"Thank you," Charles mumbled, and the woman exited the church.

He wanted to break away. He didn't think he could shake another hand. But somehow he made himself stay until the last person had passed through the front doors.

By then, he'd made up his mind. He'd ask for Tiresia's protection again so he could save Kyle from Victor. He had no idea how he would manage to do that. But somehow, he must. Whatever kind of being Kyle was, he loved him. And if pursuing him meant leaving behind the priesthood, then so be it. After all, he'd given God everything, and God had abandoned him. God had left him vulnerable first to Tiresia, then to Victor himself. Tiresia had led him to illicit love. Victor had stolen that love away—by an act of seduction. Charles felt tortured by the memory of the look of defeat in Kyle's eyes as Kyle stood at the bedroom door, looking down at Victor and him entwined in the sheets.

After Charles had removed his vestments, he left the church and walked to Rampart. At Dr. Beauchamp's house, he tried the front door. Of course it was locked. And wooden shutters covered all the windows. He crossed the street and made his way to St. Louis Cemetery. He passed through the gates, open for Sunday visitors, and wound through the tombs to the place he'd last seen her. The iron door was secure now.

"I want the power back," he whispered. "Please come and speak to me. I'll be waiting for you."

That night, he returned to the cemetery. Climbing over the gates, he went to her mausoleum, unlocking the door with his pick and shining a pen flashlight inside. It was empty. He closed the door and wandered through the dark crypts, silently invoking Tiresia's name, hoping to see her at every turn, praying that she would appear and grant him his request. But there was no sign of her. Finally, he gave up.

Leaving the cemetery, he headed for a bar on Bourbon Street, where he drank three beers before going home and crashing on the bed where Victor had conquered him. As he lay there, he imagined Victor's hard body stretched over him. He imagined the metallic taste on Victor's tongue—like a copper penny. *Blood*, he said in his mind.

Suddenly he bolted up in bed. "No!" he shouted. With or without Tiresia's protection, he couldn't relinquish Kyle to Victor. He didn't know how to rescue him, but he had to try.

Charles got up, threw on his clothes, and scrambled down to the courtyard where he boarded the Vespa. Flying out the front gate, he nearly collided with a car. The driver laid on the horn, but Charles barely registered the sound as he raced toward the Garden District. Stupidly, he wore no coat in the cool, damp night. But as he sped along Royal, warm with liquor, the chilly wind kept him alert.

He stopped outside the gates of the Greek Revival mansion, his heart thudding in his chest. He pressed the doorbell near the gate and waited. Through the iron pales he saw the front door of the mansion open. Kyle stood there, a dark silhouette against firelight glowing within the house. He must have touched the gate activator because the gate swung slowly open. As Charles advanced, Kyle's face became distinguishable and Charles stopped on the stairs, suddenly leery. There was something very different about Kyle. All traces of hopelessness had left him. He stared confidently, even fearlessly, at Charles, his skin more luminescent than ever.

"You're afraid of me," Kyle said, amused.

"You're different."

Kyle laughed. "I'm like him now."

"What do you mean?" Charles said, alarmed.

"You know what I mean."

"No, I don't!" Charles wouldn't let himself believe what Kyle was suggesting, that Victor had transformed him into a ghoulish predator.

"I'm a vampire, Charles," Kyle said, simply.

Charles stared at him, too shocked to respond.

Kyle laughed again, in a way that Charles had never heard before, with a certain cold amusement. "You think I would have run away with you? While I still needed him? How could I have? Now I can do what I want. Why don't you come in? It's chilly out here."

Kyle withdrew into the house. Stunned, Charles mechanically climbed the stairs and followed Kyle into the large front room. He found Kyle standing by the blazing fireplace.

"Close the door," Kyle said.

Charles did as instructed and turned back to Kyle.

Kyle motioned to him. "Don't be afraid. Sit down."

Charles took a seat on a plush burgundy sofa.

Kyle sat across from him in an overstuffed armchair upholstered in the same damask fabric. He was dressed all in black, his shirt turned back at the sleeves and unbuttoned halfway down his pale, muscular chest. His face, still in shadow, seemed expressionless—beautiful but frighteningly livid.

"Why?" Charles finally whispered, beginning to register the truth—and his profound loss.

Kyle's cool detachment melted now. He gazed earnestly at Charles. "You think I've given up, don't you? You think Victor has won, and now I'm his forever. You're wrong. I'm finally free, to do what I want, to who I want. He can't control me anymore, Charles! No one can. Not even your God."

"*My* God?" Charles retorted. "He's your God, too!"

Kyle shrugged, as though the point were moot. "I'm no one's

pawn now. That's what I'm saying. As a thrall I lived in limbo, not in Victor's world and not your world." He sighed, exasperated at Charles's obtuseness. "You don't have to understand it. You just have to believe that now I'm free to love you. If you'll have me. Just the way I am."

"Of course I love you. That's why I'm here. I came to fight for you."

Kyle smiled. "Thanks."

Charles didn't know whether to be relieved or horrified. Kyle had chosen him. But in doing so, had he lost salvation?

"What's it like?" Charles finally said. He had the strange feeling a person has when meeting an old, passionate lover many years later, groping to relate outside the familiar patterns of intimacy and at the same time resisting the effort.

"Indescribable. If I'd known how it would be, I sure as hell wouldn't have spent my time groveling at the feet of Christ. What a waste! It feels good to be immortal. Invincible. Not one damn thing can scare me." Kyle reached for a gold box on the table near him, pulled out a cigarette, and lit it. He noticed Charles's surprise. "Oh, this?" He glanced at the cigarette. "Why not? It's not like it'll kill me." He grinned mischievously.

This new hard sensuality aroused Charles, but he still felt the tenderness that he had experienced for the confused, innocent Kyle. Maybe because the new hard exterior meant Kyle had abandoned his deepest hopes. But if they had been groundless, anyway, shouldn't Charles be happy for him?

"I'm a vampire, Charles. A vampire!" Kyle shot out a puff of smoke. "What you see now is what you'll always see. A thirty-year-old man. With power. I'll never scrape and bow again."

"So Christ . . ."

"What about him? Joshu. That's who he is. For the past four

years Victor has told me about him. He had his chance for love. He turned it down. For that he was crowned Messiah."

Charles' had a knee-jerk reaction to the blasphemy. But he reminded himself that Christ had betrayed him, too.

"You sure as hell owe him nothing. Christ. All of your strength came from the world of Evil!" Kyle exaggerated the word, wriggling his fingers in mock trembling.

"I'm through with the priesthood," Charles conceded. "I love you, Kyle."

"I hope so." Kyle rose. "Come on."

"Where?"

"You'll see."

Kyle approached Charles and grabbed him by the hand. Kyle's flesh was cold as a stone. Kyle pulled Charles up and stared into his eyes, Kyle's own gray irises scintillating. He kissed Charles on the lips, and Charles wrapped his arms around him.

Kyle jerked away. "Don't cling to me. Not yet."

Charles shivered at Kyle's allusion to the words of Christ to Mary Magdalene outside his tomb on Easter morning. *Don't cling to me. I'm no longer in your world.*

Docilely, Charles let Kyle lead him out into the night. Hand in hand, they strolled down one of the grand streets of the Garden District, where several antebellum mansions stood. The electricity had still not been restored to the streetlights, and in the moonless night, the darkness was profound.

Kyle stopped before one of the old mansions. A gallery above the portico stretched the width of the house. He inhaled deeply and moaned.

"What is it?" Charles said.

"Blood."

Kyle led the way up the front walk, nodding for Charles to follow, but he remained fixed in place. Kyle returned and grabbed
him by the arm.

"What are you doing?" Charles said.

"What do you think? I have to feed."

"No!" Charles recoiled at the thought.

"If you want to love me, you have to face this. Now."

Kyle's words sounded like a dare rather than a plea, but Charles
decided to hear them as a plea all the same. Despite himself, he
yielded, following Kyle around the house, through a gate, and to a
set of French doors in back of the house. All was dark within. Kyle
laid his ear on the glass and listened. He tried the door, and finding it locked, pushed with incredible force, though barely exerting
himself. The door broke through the dead bolt. The noise made
Kyle hesitate, but satisfied that no one stirred within, he proceeded. In the darkness, Charles could make out a large room
with high ceilings, packed with heavy furnishings. A moldy odor
hung in the air. Oil portraits hung on one wall, the subjects hardly
discernible.

They proceeded down a hallway to the staircase. Kyle began
climbing. Charles's heart raced as he followed. In the upstairs
hall, Kyle raised his head and sniffed the air. There were several
closed doors, but two were ajar. He softly closed one of them and
approached the other, nodding to Charles. Charles could not
believe what he was doing, invading a house, preying on its occupants. But he followed Kyle into the room, where a nightlight
glowed in a wall outlet. In the center of the room rose a canopy
bed. A wall of shelves held stuffed animals. In one corner sat a
large Victorian dollhouse.

Kyle's breathing grew loud and quick as he moved to the bed.

My God, Charles thought, *it's a little girl.* He could make out the tiny face on the pillow. The girl lay on her side, her plump hand near her face.

"No," he whispered. "She's just a child."

Kyle shrugged and bent over the pillow of the sleeping girl. Charles started to retreat, but Kyle clutched his arm with the strength of a vise.

"You watch this," he said in a low, gravelly voice that Charles had never heard.

Futilely Charles tried to wrench his arm away, but finally gave in, still in Kyle's hold as Kyle lowered his mouth to the girl's throat. Charles wanted to close his eyes, but he made himself watch. He had to see.

The little girl let out a brief, sharp cry, then became quiet as Kyle siphoned her blood. Suddenly there were footsteps in the hall. Someone appeared at the door. "Matty!" The strained voice belonged to an elderly woman. When she saw the two intruders she gasped and ran to the bed. "Get away from her!" she cried. "Matty!"

She grabbed the little girl and tried to scoop her up, but Kyle snatched her away, picking up the child and placing her in Charles's arms. Charles's impulse was to whisk the little girl out of the room and down the stairs, but he also wanted to save the woman. When she made her way around the bed to rescue the girl, Kyle clutched her by the throat, lifting her off the floor.

"Let her go!" Charles shouted.

Kyle glared at him, and as the woman tugged desperately at his hands, he intensified his grip. She finally went limp, and he dropped her on the floor.

Panicking, Charles rushed to the door with the little girl. But when he reached it, Kyle stood there, blocking his path, as though he'd transported himself by thought alone.

"You're not gonna hurt her!" Charles said.

"Why should I want to? She'll remember nothing about us. We're safe. You think I'm a cold-blooded killer?"

"Yes!" Charles said, fearfully.

Kyle laughed. "So now you see who you love. Put her on the bed. She'll recover."

Charles felt torn. He didn't want to leave the girl, but he wanted to take Kyle as far away from her as possible. Kyle turned and left the room. When Charles heard him descending the stairs, he finally carried the little girl back to the bed. He'd call the police when he got home and have them come rescue her.

When he reached the street outside the house, Charles saw blood on Kyle's mouth. A violent wave of nausea suddenly passed through him. He leaned against a tree and retched.

"You'll get used to it," Kyle said.

Charles glanced up and watched Kyle light a cigarette. "You've turned into him," he said. "You're a monster, too."

Kyle shrugged. "Food chain. You've heard of it. This is my nature now."

Charles straightened up and wiped his face with his sleeve.

"Still love me?" Kyle said.

"You don't have to do this."

"Really?" Kyle chuckled. "You think I can get a day job?"

"You don't have to be a monster."

Kyle's expression turned serious now. "I had to kill that woman. I had no choice."

Charles suddenly turned and moved toward the house.

"Where are you going?" Kyle said.

"To call 911. Someone has to take care of the little girl."

Kyle once again appeared from nowhere and blocked his path. "Let it go."

"If I call from the house, they won't be able to trace us. Don't you want to help her?"

Kyle did not yield. He stood with his arms crossed. "She'll be found."

"If you don't let me do this, I'll call on my cell. Unless you plan to kill me."

Kyle yielded, letting him pass.

Inside the house, Charles found a phone in the large room inside the back doors. He picked up the receiver and called 911, blurting out that a woman had suffered a stroke. He provided the address but instantly hung up when the female operator began asking questions.

Then he went up to the little girl's bedroom. He switched on a lamp by the bed and examined the child. She slept peacefully, her head turned to one side on the pillow, exposing the red wounds on her tender throat. He felt her hand. It was warm with life. He moved to the other side of the bed and surveyed the white-haired woman, lying on the floor, wrapped in a rose bathrobe. Her open eyes stared at the ceiling. Her mouth gaped, the tongue visible. He imagined her grandchild or whoever the girl was awaking to find the old woman like this.

When he turned around, Kyle stood there, leaning against the wall, his arms folded.

"How can you change this much?" Charles said.

Kyle raised his cigarette to his lips. He exhaled a stream of smoke. "I'll ask you again—do you still love me?"

Charles glanced at the little girl on the bed. Reluctant to leave her but needing to flee before paramedics or police came, he left the room, ran down the stairs, and left the house. As he walked, he expected Kyle to appear once again in his path. But there was no sign of him all the way back to the mansion.

He boarded the Vespa and raced back to the Quarter. Entering a bar on Bourbon Street, he gulped down three shots of whiskey. He managed to stumble home to bed. "God forgive me," he muttered before falling asleep.

13

Outside the mausoleum, Victor drew Kyle close and kissed him. The chirping of birds belied the darkness. Dawn rapidly approached.

"You're warm," Kyle said.

"No. You're feeling the sun's radiation. Your flesh stings. Doesn't it?"

"Let's get inside."

"You go." Victor released him. "I told you—I plan to see the sunrise."

"And what if you're wrong?" Kyle said with chilling indifference.

Victor mused a moment over the new Kyle: cocky, cold, unafraid. This arrogance aroused him. It promised competition that rallied the blood—and lovemaking as passionate as it been the last few nights. Uncontested domination had its charms, but a fight for domination was exhilarating. He leaned forward and whispered in Kyle's ear. "It's good to no longer need me. Isn't it? To be my equal, finally. That's everything, Kyle. Forget him. Now we can have a real life together."

"Maybe," Kyle said, teasingly.

Victor turned from him and surveyed the graying sky. "I'm

not wrong. Every atom of my body tells me I'm impervious to the first light now. I'm a vampire maker. I plan to look into the face of the sun and dare it to burn me."

"Good luck," Kyle said, patting Victor's shoulder. "If you're gone when I rise, New Orleans will belong to me. At least in the night." He entered the mausoleum, pulling the iron door shut behind him.

Victor exited the cemetery and rose into the warming air, lighting near the river. On the riverwalk, he leaned against a lamppost, looking eastward across the water to the pink light cutting into the dark sky. When was the last time he had watched the sunrise? Had it been one of the many times he had wasted the night in one of Jerusalem's brothels before tramping back to his military headquarters? Or had it been the night he and Joshu had spent on the Sea of Galilee, where they had fallen asleep gazing up at the stars, only to be awakened by the rising sun?

Adrenaline surged through him now, the way it had in the chariot as he waited for the race to begin at the Circus Maximus—the race among Roman officers, of course, not the slave races conducted for the masses.

Suddenly the horizon flamed. Victor stood erect, away from the lamppost, to greet his burning opponent. The sun's radiation stirred his flesh now. Formerly, he would have writhed in the stinging rays. Now they invigorated him, like the intense spray of a shower or a stimulating rubdown. He lifted his face to gather up the light, closing his eyes at first, then opening them to stare into the face of dawn.

The bright rim emerged and rose. Victor's chest heaved. The sun climbed higher, a full round orb of heat. And the hot tears of victory filled his eyes.

His skin suddenly began to sting. His strength waned. So this was the point of surrender after making two vampires. What might it be after making a dozen?

He could not afford to ponder the matter now. His flesh warned him to seek his resting place. He relinquished the spot reluctantly, strolling toward one of the buildings near the riverbank. In the window of a building, an image startled him. It was an image he had not seen for two thousand years: his own face and body. Being a vampire maker had returned this ability to see his reflection. He stared at his handsome features and form, grinning at the sight before rising at the speed of thought and soaring to his tomb.

On awakening that night, Victor found Kyle standing over his coffin. "Are you surprised that I survived?" he said.

Kyle shrugged.

"Are you happy?"

Kyle nodded. He turned and exited the mausoleum.

Victor rose and followed him outside.

"I want to feed," Kyle said.

"It's like being a drug addict, isn't it?" Victor said, touching Kyle's cheek. "That's how it is at first. With time, your self-control will grow. You'll be able to forgo feeding for days."

"You can forgo if you want," Kyle said. Then he grinned mischievously. "Or we can feast together."

Victor decided to humor Kyle's gluttonous urge—clear on his face. They began their banquet at a nearby house. Kyle had watched the middle-aged woman who came and went from the house and knew she lived alone. On her front porch, they heard the television inside. Kyle rang the bell. When the woman answered the door, he shoved her inside and threw her to the floor, lunging at her neck before she had time to struggle.

Victor watched him drink, then joined him, stopping before the fatal point.

"Stop, or she won't make it," Victor said, tugging at Kyle's shoulder.

Kyle pulled his mouth away, struggling to restrain himself. Finally, he got up on his knees and knelt over her as though he were praying.

"She'll recover," Victor assured him.

"I almost went too far," Kyle said.

"But you didn't."

"No. Not this time."

"Don't worry. In time, you'll develop self-control."

"Until then?"

"The law of the jungle, I'm afraid. Let's go."

The next victim was a man carting his garbage to the curb, then an old couple walking their dog. Before midnight, Kyle had feasted on a dozen victims, finally vomiting the excess of blood.

Victor indulged Kyle in his feasting for the next few nights, also indulging the prodigious lust produced by the violence. It was as though the desires that Kyle had repressed throughout his human life exploded within him. He craved touch. He craved passion. Victor took pleasure in Kyle's new zest.

Meanwhile, his own powers grew. Each morning he walked in the sunlight a few minutes more than he had on the previous day. With great anticipation, he awaited the day when he could stand beneath a blazing noon sun. He imagined his freedom to move about by day—managing his business affairs, traveling, abandoning altogether the dark, moldy crypt.

His sense of invincibility surged in him like a mighty tide. If he eventually conquered the most threatening enemy, the sunlight, perhaps the stake—fatally dangerous even in the hands of a weak coward—would also be rendered useless by his power. What then would be left to fear?

A strategy for amassing power suggested itself to him. He could create a legion of thralls, convincing them one by one to accept the life of a vampire. Creatures in limbo had much more incentive than humans to accept the terms of such a transformation. Of course, he would have dominion over these neophyte predators, just as he had had dominion over Kyle. The realm of Victor Decimus, Victor the Invincible!

Naked and excited, Victor and Kyle wrestled on their bed. Kyle playfully twisted Victor's arm behind him, biting his ear, then licking the back of his neck. Victor couldn't take the teasing anymore. He rolled over, pinning Kyle to the mattress with his body. Then lifting Kyle's legs, he heaved them over his shoulder and plunged into him. Kyle moaned in pain, then pleasure. After they'd both climaxed, Victor kissed Kyle and lay on his back next to him. The drapes were open, and moonlight washed over them. For a long while, their hearts pounding, they basked quietly in the silver light.

Finally Kyle rolled toward Victor. "This is why I agreed to be transformed," he said.

"Sex?" Victor laughed. "Being human didn't stop you from that, if I recall!"

"But I never had it without guilt."

Victor shook his head. "Pity."

"And I never had it with love. It's all I ever wanted. Now I'm free to have it."

Victor was moved by the admission. He reached for Kyle's hand and kissed it, pressing it tenderly to his own heart.

After more silence, Kyle said, "What was it like for you? In the first years after your transformation."

"Glorious," Victor said. "I wanted to see other parts of the world. I traveled to the East. Asia intrigued me. The warlords and their flashing sabers. The delightful protocols and hierarchies." An image of a particularly stunning warlord came to Victor's mind. He was a giant of a man with long blue-black hair who had just stepped into his bath. Victor had stolen into his house, aglow with lanterns, and crept up behind him. As he grabbed the man by the throat, the warrior fought with admirable strength, his biceps like mountains and his hands like vises. But under Victor's will, he quickly went limp. Victor drew his prodigious, dripping body from the tub, gazing on it lustfully before nuzzling his throat and sinking teeth into the beautiful flesh.

"You didn't feel like a prisoner of the tomb?" Kyle continued.

The remark drew Victor from his reverie. "Your life is too new to resist such a meager boundary."

"I hate creeping back at night to the mausoleum."

"But you crave your resting place."

"Yes. And I hate it."

Victor laughed. He rolled toward Kyle and stroked his chest. "Where did all your religious submission go? It might be worth your while to recover some of it."

"Never." Kyle removed Victor's hand from his chest. He rolled onto his back, drew his hands behind his head, and stared at the ceiling.

Victor admired Kyle's handsome face and muscular physique.

"Some of the greatest saints were the worst sinners," Kyle said. "Augustine, for example. He was a pagan. He had an illegitimate child. In *The Confessions,* he goes on and on about how wicked he was. And Constantine. He was a ruthless emperor before his deathbed conversion."

"Hardly ruthless." Victor remembered the first Christian emperor well—addressing the masses in the square below his palace on the Capitoline Hill in Rome. Constantine's reign had been nearly over when Victor had returned to Rome from the East. "He couldn't hold a candle to Caligula."

"At any rate," Kyle continued, "Augustine and Constantine had their fun first, before their big conversions. I've saved mine for last. The last will be first!"

"Why not?" Victor caressed Kyle's chest. "But not here. I want to leave this city. I'm tired of the rot and devastation. I want some opulence. Maybe the French Riviera. Maybe Venice." Victor had been toying with the idea for some time now. He had been in the New World long enough. He craved the sophistication and charm of Europe.

Kyle sat up. He looked alarmed. "No. We'll stay here."

Kyle's vehemence surprised Victor. "Hasn't your transformation made you want adventure? The world is at your feet. Why stay in this garbage heap?"

"I don't know," Kyle said evasively, glancing away from Victor. Then he added unconvincingly, "I'm used to it. It's where I was born. Into this life."

Victor studied him with suspicion. "It's him. Isn't it? You want to be near the priest. So you haven't changed completely. That's too bad." Angry, Victor got up and started to dress. "Because he has to go. He's a danger to me. I'm surprised he hasn't tried to act yet."

Kyle's eyes widened in alarm. "How is he a danger?"

"How do you think? And he's a danger to you, too." Victor

chose a pair of gabardine trousers from the mahogany wardrobe and slipped them on.

"He would never try to hurt me. And why should he try to hurt you?"

"He's a priest," Victor said. "He thinks I'm Satan." He could see Kyle start to protest, and he cut the younger man off. "Don't tell me he's sworn off his Christ now. That's today's mood. Tomorrow he might repent of his blasphemy. And besides, I've taken you away from him."

Kyle was agitated now. He reached for a cigarette on the nightstand and lit it. "All right. Then let's just leave the city."

Victor chuckled. "Your affection for him is touching. We will leave the city. And I will take care of him." Victor turned to close the wardrobe door. When he turned back, Kyle was not in the bed. He now stood in front of the door, having transported himself in an instant. "You don't imagine you can stop me?" Victor said.

Kyle glared at him in reply.

An impulse to attack him flared up in Victor, and then suddenly died. When he looked at Kyle now, he remembered the original allure of creating a mate who shared his nature. For an instant he remembered his love for Paul. The scene of their wedding flashed before his eyes. They had stood hand in hand, two beings with the same nature, before the baldachino of the candlelit basilica that they had invaded by night to exchange their vows. Paul's hazel eyes, the soft, tender eyes of an artist, gazed shyly at him. The world lay at their feet. But finally they had parted for the sake of survival. In his bitterness, Victor had hardened. In his early years as a predator, his heart was merely cold. With his separation from Paul, it had frozen. Before him now lay the possibility of feeling it beat once again. Power enticed him, but at least one be-ing must share it if he wanted love.

Victor approached Kyle. "Remember our dream?" he said gently, touching Kyle's cheek. "Our life together, through the centuries, equal beings ruling the night together. You could never have that with him. He could never understand your na-ture."

"Equal? I'll never see daylight again. Not like you."

"We're still the same. No other being in the world can under-stand you the way I do."

Kyle yielded, his body relaxing, his eyes softening. "Do you love me?"

"Yes." It felt good to finally say it.

Kyle seemed pleased. Then a cloud overcame him. "But I'll never replace *him*. Joshu."

"Why should you want to? He's just a phantom."

"A phantom you've chased for two thousand years."

"Chased! I have no access to his world. He appears to me and offers his redemption. It's his wishful thinking. Even if I wanted it, we inhabit different realms."

Kyle seemed to consider his words. Then he raised his chin and stared boldly into Victor's eyes. "I lived my whole life as a slave to a God the Church invented. I was a slave to the Church. Then I became a slave to you. You don't know what that's like. You've never submitted to anyone a day in your life. Why shouldn't I live like a king now? Giving orders instead of taking them? Why shouldn't I have my own thrall? Don't kill the priest. Let me have him."

Victor scrutinized Kyle's face. He saw deception there. "You just want to save him. If you love him, you'll let me take care of him. Better for him to be in his heaven than trapped in a world he loathes. But I don't have to tell you that."

"He's given up on heaven. Christ abandoned him."

Victor laughed. "I wouldn't put much stock in his blasphemy. He's just licking his wounds. His disillusionment is temporary. He's resilient. And courageous. He will not be a doting thrall. You'll eventually want to destroy him."

"Or offer him what you offered me."

Victor laughed at the idea of it. "You were desperate. He won't be."

Kyle looked troubled. "Why should I believe you?"

"You don't have the stomach to be a solitary predator. Of course you will survive, but . . ." Victor felt no need to finish. He could see that Kyle knew he was right. "And if in the future you feel inclined to part from me, well then, what's to prevent it? You can create a thrall whenever you want."

Kyle yielded, his whole body relaxing, the fierceness of his gaze melting away. "Why does he have to die?"

Victor drew near Kyle and embraced him, whispering in his ear. "See how tender-hearted you are? It is better this way. He's a danger to me. He instills self-doubt in you." Victor drew away from Kyle and grabbed his arm. "Come on. We'll get it over with. I'll do everything."

"Then do it," Kyle said with resignation. "Why do I have to go?"

"You have to see this through. You have to take part. Otherwise you'll resent me."

"Won't I resent you more if I'm forced to watch?"

"I won't force you. But being there with me will strengthen our bond. That's what you want, isn't it? It's why you entered this new life, you said. To find love." Victor kissed him on the lips. "Now, come on."

Docilely, Kyle followed Victor down the stairs and out to the dark street. The night felt still and damp. They walked to the Quarter, Victor expounding on the future he envisioned. Travels across the globe. Palaces. Orgies. Thralls at their command, then new peers, one vampire at a time. Gradually they would realize all the power so feared by the Dark Kingdom.

He told Kyle how pleasing he found the changes in his erstwhile thrall: Kyle's boldness, his strength. His hardening would put Kyle in good stead for the life he had accepted. Kyle seemed to take heart, and Victor was glad.

When they reached the priest's residence, Victor broke through the gate. They climbed up to the priest's apartment, but they discovered only dark, empty rooms.

"He's at the cathedral," Kyle surmised, as though the darkness had whispered Charles's whereabouts to him.

"Indeed?" Victor sneered. "So much for his renunciation of God."

They set out for the church. When they arrived, they found the door on the side of the cathedral unlocked, and they entered.

The sanctuary candle burned at the high altar in the chancel, and votive candles flickered in the racks near the front pews. In the tongues of light, Victor easily discerned the priest, kneeling on the marble floor before the tabernacle. Victor started to climb the steps to the sanctuary, but Kyle reflexively grabbed his arm.

"Let me do this," Victor said. "It will be over in a second."

Kyle hesitated, but finally nodded, apparently determined to resist his impulses, and Victor proceeded.

Aware of their presence now, the priest shot to his feet and faced Victor fearfully. Then he looked beyond him at Kyle, who stood near the communion rail. "What are you doing?"

When Kyle did not respond, Victor turned to catch his

expression. Kyle was staring painfully at Charles, but with his jaw set, as though he had consented to putting a sick pet out of its misery.

"My God!" Charles blurted, realizing their intentions. "How can you do this, Kyle?"

Kyle took a step forward, as though he wanted to go to Charles, but he stopped himself. "Get it over with," he said to Victor.

"I love you!" Charles implored, panic in his voice. "I don't care what you are."

"It's no use," Kyle said.

"He's absolutely right." At the speed of thought, Victor had transported himself to the tabernacle. He now stood face to face with Charles. When Charles made a move to run, Victor lunged at him, throwing him to the marble floor and pinning back his arms. Adrenaline raced through Victor, and he salivated, his fangs growing. But as he opened his mouth wide to attack the priest, he felt himself being yanked away. Suddenly Kyle was straddling him, pinning back his arms. Victor smiled, admiring the strength of his creation. But his own strength was superior, and he thrust Kyle from him and sprang to his feet to confront him. "Don't be foolish," he said. "You can't stop me."

The priest scrambled up and began running for the door. Victor willed him to stop, and he instantly fell, paralyzed, on the sanctuary steps.

Kyle lunged at Victor again, choking him. Victor pried Kyle's hands from his throat and shoved the younger man against the tabernacle. Kyle flew at him, knocking him to the floor and landing on top of Victor. But then Kyle's ferocity suddenly gave way to desperation. "Please, let him live," he pleaded.

His chest heaving from the struggle, Victor stared into Kyle's gray eyes. He felt no mercy, but a realization came to him in that moment. If he destroyed the priest against Kyle's wishes, he risked losing Kyle as his lover. Once again, he would be alone. Worse yet, he might gain a dangerous enemy. With time, Kyle would surely come to his senses and finally consent to the priest's destruction. And when he did, Victor would carry it out on his own. He would not make the mistake of making Kyle watch.

"All right," Victor conceded. "For now."

Kyle scrutinized his face, incredulous of Victor's sincerity. But apparently he saw something in Victor's gaze that satisfied him on the point, and he released Victor. With an act of will, Victor in turn released Charles, and the priest ran out of the church.

14

Charles paced his apartment, clutching the broomstick he'd whittled to a point with his Swiss Army knife. If Victor came for him, he'd be ready. He wouldn't wait for Victor to make the first move. The moment he crossed the threshold, Charles would lunge at his heart.

A sound on the balcony made Charles jump. He'd latched the big shutters over the windows—they were really doors with louvers, the kind lots of houses had in New Orleans. So he couldn't peek out to see if Victor was there. But he waited. Silence. It went on for several moments, and he sighed in relief.

He lowered the broomstick and continued pacing, oblivious to the TV voices of the *Law and Order* cast, now in the middle of a courtroom scene.

What had he gotten himself into? And what did he do now? How could he go on as a priest—eaten up as he was by a sense of betrayal? Not only hadn't Christ cured him, He'd abandoned him to evil. And now he was in love with a cold-blooded predator.

But a predator who had saved his life. Kyle must love him. That thought brought Charles an incredible sense of joy.

The sound of footsteps was unmistakeable now. Charles approached the door, the makeshift stake raised, awaiting the intruder.

There was a knock, perfectly innocuous. Then a voice. "Charles!" It was Pete.

Charles unlocked the door and pulled Pete into the apartment, securing the door behind him.

"What's going on?" Pete said. "You didn't answer your cell phone." He wore a black sweatshirt and black jeans that made him look tall and skinny as a pole. He glanced with alarm at the stake in Charles's hand. "What in the hell is that for?"

"You shouldn't be here," Charles said, evasively.

"Tell me what's happening," Pete demanded.

"I want you to go back home."

"Tell me!"

Charles could see it was no use trying to get rid of Pete. His dark eyes were full of determination.

"All right," Charles yielded. "Sit down." He motioned to the couch.

Pete sat down, and Charles perched on the edge of the couch next to him, ready to jump up if he had to. He switched off the TV with the remote. "Kyle's like him now," he said. "A vampire." As he told Pete about Kyle's transformation and Victor's attack, his eyes kept darting toward the door, behind Pete's head.

Pete listened in horror. After Charles had finished, he sat in stunned silence. "So Kyle saved you?" he finally said.

Charles shrugged. "For now."

"He wouldn't let anything happen to you."

"No," Charles admitted. "Not if he could help it. But he can't control Victor's every move."

"But if Victor cares for Kyle. If he loves him . . ." Pete hesitated, as if he suddenly realized the indelicacy of saying this to Charles. "I'm sorry. I know how you feel about Kyle. But if he's like Victor now . . . well, what kind of future could you have together?"

The truth of Pete's words felt like a knife in Charles's gut. Rallying himself, he tightened his grip on the broomstick and, in that moment, made a decision. "I'm going to do it!"

"Do what?" Pete looked confused.

Charles shook his head, dismissing the question. "It's too complicated to explain."

"Come on, Charles!"

"Not now. I'll tell you later."

Pete scrutinized Charles's face for an answer. Then he glanced at the stake and put two and two together. "You're going after Victor," he said, accusingly.

"He's already dead, Pete," Charles said defensively. "I wouldn't be committing murder."

"But if he's not really a threat . . ."

"Why do you keep saying that?" Exasperated, Charles got up, unlocked the door, and stepped out onto the balcony. His resolution made him feel fearless now. Let Victor come if he wanted. The air was cool and damp. Charles tapped the iron rail with the stick as he peered down into the dark courtyard. He heard Pete's step behind him.

"You're right," Pete conceded. "You gotta protect yourself."

"Damn right." Charles tapped the rail again, telling himself that self-defense was his only motive—or the only one that mattered. It didn't matter that he hated Victor for taking Kyle away from him, or that he wanted to punish Kyle, or that he had a wild dream that he and Kyle could have a future together without Victor.

"When are you gonna do it?" Pete said solemnly.

"Soon." Rap, rap.

"I'll go with you."

"No!" Charles turned to his brother. "I'm doing it alone."

"Come on, Charles," Pete reasoned. "You shouldn't do this alone."

"I said no!" The last thing Charles wanted was to plant in his little brother's mind the indelible memory of plunging a stake into the heart of a living corpse. "Please, Pete," he said, softening his tone. "Let me do this alone."

Pete saw there was no use arguing. He finally yielded, looking down at the courtyard. "Your life won't be the same," he said.

"It already isn't," Charles said.

They didn't talk much longer. There was nothing left to say. Charles finally sent Pete home and climbed into bed. It was after midnight. He needed his sleep for what he had to do—which he'd carry out at noon, when the strong sun guaranteed that Victor would be powerless. Before that, he'd keep his usual appointments. What else could he do for now?

He slept fitfully. In the middle of the night a violent dream involving screams and being pursed and a bloody corpse woke him up. He thought he sensed a presence in his bedroom. He began to reassure himself that he was confusing reality with his dream, when an unmistakeably real figure moved in the shadows. He snatched the stake lying at his side and jumped out of bed, facing the figure.

"You called for me." The voice belonged to Tiresia. She stepped toward Charles, and a strange luminescence suddenly made her visible. She stared languidly at him from beneath the hood of her robe, her eyelids glittering with gold.

Charles lowered the stake. "I don't need you anymore."

"I can protect you from him again. I will, if you let him live."

Charles stared at her, taken aback. "You want him to live?"

"He's my creation!" Tiresia spoke with a surprising tenderness. "I want him to live."

"But he's a vampire maker. I thought your world was paying some kind of price for it. That's what Kyle told me."

"Yes. That's why the neophyte must die."

"You mean Kyle?" Charles blurted. "You plan to kill him?"

"Because he's one of my own, I should want more than anything for him to thrive in his new nature. But if he does, we inhabitants of the Dark Kingdom shall continue to pay a grave penalty. Our lives will remain frozen. The cosmic order requires the balance of light and darkness, victim and predator. This new association between vampires is forbidden."

"But Kyle told me that Victor already made another vampire," Charles argued. "Victor left him so they both could live. They aren't together, so there is no association. Why can't that happen again? Kyle could leave Victor. That would take care of the universal law or whatever you called it." Kyle leaving Victor, with him— that was Charles's secret hope.

"I assure you, their separation would not satisfy us. Victor has established a precedent. He won't stop now. He's become a vampire maker." Tiresia hesitated. "And so I require your assistance."

"What do you mean?" Charles said. "If you don't want me to take care of Victor . . ." Suddenly his confusion gave way to horror as he guessed her meaning. "Jesus!"

Tiresia saw he understood her intention. "If I could destroy him, I would. I don't care for this puny neophyte. But we cannot destroy our own."

"Thank God," Charles said, incredibly relieved.

"You have foolish ideas," Tiresia snapped. "You believe this new vampire will be yours. You believe he's the same being that he was before his transformation. You are wrong. See for yourself if he will love you or if you can love him. I doubt you can love a demon. The best you can do is save him. Send him to your God and his heaven. Or have you completely abandoned your beliefs?"

"Go to hell," Charles said, enraged by her judgment. "And why should I believe anything you say about God?"

Tiresia shrugged. "Believe what you will. But you know I can cure you once more of the affliction you despise. I can cure you once and for all. It's all you've wanted. Isn't it? To be a pure priest of God. Imagine your bliss. All the good you could do."

Charles's heart leapt at the idea. He was surprised how strong the longing remained in him to be cured, despite Pete's reassurance that his nature wasn't somehow twisted. Still, he loved Kyle. He could never harm him.

Tiresia narrowed her eyes, surmising his thoughts. "I urge you to reconsider. And when you do, your reward awaits you." With those words, her luminosity faded and she vanished.

Distraught, Charles slept no more that night. Tiresia's offer played and replayed in his mind. He imagined standing over Kyle's coffin, instead of Victor's, positioning the stake over his heart. No—cure or no cure, he could never harm Kyle. He'd rather take his chances loving him and being sent to hell himself for all eternity.

At dawn he finally got up and went to his office. Sitting at his desk, he filled out marriage license forms for couples whose weddings he'd officiated at. He kept looking out the window into the sky, gauging how far the sun had risen, and counting the hours until noon.

At ten, a parishioner came to the office, requesting him to bless her home in the Gentilly neighborhood. She was fifty or so, with very clear olive skin and bright green eyes that matched a strand in her mottled sweater. She taught in a Catholic grade school.

"I'm moving back in. I don't care if I'm the only person back on the block. I know it's a big inconvenience, Father. But it would mean so much to Jack and me."

An errand of mercy was the last thing Charles wanted to do in his hyped-up state. But he couldn't refuse the woman. On his Vespa, he followed her car to the working-class neighborhood, where virtually every house stood empty. The owners of some of the houses had taken care to return long enough to board up the windows. And blue government-issued tarps covered a few roofs in the process of being repaired. But other houses seemed permanently abandoned, their yards full of debris carried by the flooding. The waterline on all the houses was just below their roofs. An overturned car sat in a median strip across from the parishioner's house. The gas station on the corner was abandoned.

A large metal container in the woman's yard bulged with ruined sheetrock, carpeting, and linoleum. Inside the house, the walls had been stripped to the studs, and sheets of new plywood formed the floor. Despite the demolition, a dank, moldy smell lingered.

Charles read a blessing from his prayer book and sprinkled the walls in the room with holy water he'd brought. The woman thanked him and tried to give him a twenty-dollar bill for his trouble. He refused it.

Before he boarded his Vespa, he gazed around the ruined street. Jesus's lament over Jerusalem came to his mind:

> Jerusalem, Jerusalem, the city that kills the prophets and stones those who are sent to it! How often have I desired to gather your children together as a hen gathers her brood. See, your house is left to you, desolate!

Did God really care about this destruction? This upheaval? Or had God caused it? And if He had, then why did Charles care about pleasing Him? Why did he still feel drawn to help this desolate community? Why did he still want to help the people here?

At a quarter till twelve, Charles splashed water on his face to calm himself and collected the tools he needed.

The day was dreary. But, invisible or not, the sun—his protector—shone above the clouds. And that was all that mattered.

He arrived at Lafayette Cemetery with steady nerves, walking purposefully to Victor's mausoleum. No visitors were in sight. He manipulated the lock with ease and entered the chamber. He considered closing the door behind him, but he needed the light and left the door ajar, risking detection by any curious visitor who might happen by. Who cared if someone saw him?

Both coffins lay before him, side by side. It was strange to think of Kyle climbing into this casket every day before sunrise. Charles couldn't resist looking at him. The priest took a deep breath to steel himself and opened the lid. Kyle's pale, luminous face greeted him, peaceful and innocent as an angel's. If his breathing had been discernible, anyone would have believed him to be sleeping. But his chest was as still as Victor's had been the first time Charles had entered this tomb. Charles mumbled a prayer and brushed Kyle's cheek tenderly. He thought of Tiresia's promise—a cure in exchange for Kyle's life. But as he peered at his beloved, he experienced no struggle in his heart between a longing for purity and the deepest love he had ever felt. He knew in that moment that love was the only thing that mattered. He couldn't bear the thought of life without Kyle.

So he moved to Victor's coffin, flung open the lid before he lost his nerve, and positioned the stake between the man's ribs, over his heart. In his violet silk shirt, Victor lay still, his face registering no danger—even though in one instant his ancient life would come to an end. A life two thousand years old, now in Charles's hands. Charles raised the hammer. He held it there a moment, hesitating—his heart drumming his own ribs—and then he let it fall again at his side. He glanced over at Kyle. So beautiful. So angelic in this state of repose.

If he really loved Kyle, how could he rob him of his only equal? His one chance for love with someone who understood his nature? And if he did destroy Victor, would Kyle ever forgive him? And could he and Kyle ever be happy—living in two different worlds?

The evil of Kyle's new world was beyond him—ghoulish predators, a Dark Kingdom, death and destruction. He searched his heart and found no call to leap into a cosmic battle with such a world. He was made for the everyday world. That's the only place he would ever do any good.

But what if Victor decided to end Charles's existence in the everyday world? Panic swelled in the priest, but then it dissipated as quickly as it had come. He had to risk an attack and hope that Kyle could protect him. Better to keep his hands free of murder, even the murder of a fiend, and enter heaven than to resort to Satan's ways and risk damnation.

"God help me," he whispered.

Calm now, and resolved, he closed Victor's coffin, and then, lingering over Kyle, closed his coffin too. He exited the tomb, securing the door behind him.

The clouds had cleared away, and a bright sun beat on him. The sun had never felt so good.

Let everything work out God's purpose. The words seemed to come from Christ, whose unmistakeable presence, Charles now realized—a presence on the bare edge of his consciousness back in the tomb—had strengthened him there. And the realization brought him hope beyond his wildest imaginings. *Love,* he heard Christ saying, *not force, will bring all creation into light.*

EPILOGUE

He seemed as real as you," Kyle said. He and Victor were strolling in the dark Garden District. A warm breeze rustled the magnolias on both sides of the street. "Joshu stood with Charles over my coffin. One of them touched my cheek."

What Kyle believed to be a dream, Victor knew to be reality. Even in his state of rest, his senses had alerted him to the presence of the two intruders in their mausoleum. But the intruders had not alarmed him. Since becoming a vampire maker, his senses had remained keen even during his sleep, and he had no doubts that with his new powers, he could now rally himself for an attack if necessary, even in his state of rest. But during the intrusion he had known that such a rally was unnecessary. He had known that one of the intruders was Joshu and—he had intuited clearly and distinctly—Joshu would allow no harm to come to him. Remembering this now gratified Victor deeply—in fact, embarrassingly so, since he hated to admit the hold Joshu exercised over him, and he decided to keep the information from Kyle. So, with a chuckle, he dismissed Kyle's "dream."

"Be careful," he said. "You'll have Joshu haunting you, the way he's haunted me."

Kyle stopped in his tracks. "That's the first time you've ever admitted that. Joshu haunting you."

"Why not? I'm in a good mood. I don't care what Joshu does or doesn't do."

Kyle undoubtedly knew the enormity of this lie. But he did not contradict him. They continued walking.

"You must have lasted a long time in the sunlight," Kyle finally said, turning to a new subject.

"Indeed." Victor felt his new power now in every atom of his body. "I stayed up until mid-morning. I stared the sun in the face."

"And then?"

"Then I wanted my rest."

They strolled past a Victorian mansion. Victor admired a sculpture of a nude discus thrower on the lawn.

"I'm ready to leave New Orleans now," Kyle said. "Why don't we go west? To San Francisco?"

Victor could see through this ploy. On another day, he might have been provoked. But yesterday's triumph over the sun made him indulgent. "You want to save him."

"If we leave here, he's no threat to you."

"But you do love him. Admit it. What does it matter to me? He's mortal. You'll forget him in a year or ten years. It's all the same to beings like us."

Kyle shrugged. "What does it matter? I've chosen *you*."

The response filled Victor with deep satisfaction. He pulled Kyle to a halt and kissed him passionately on the lips.

A man with a dog on a leash approached them ahead. They both thought the same thing without saying it. Eager to feed, they kept their eyes on their prey. When he was close enough, Victor willed the dog to be silent and pounced on the man. He and Kyle drank until they were sated, leaving the man to awaken on the sidewalk.

"Do you think we've seen the last of Tiresia?" Kyle said after a while.

"No."

"Does that bother you?"

"Why should it? I'll enjoy playing her game. I'll always be the winner."

"Are you sure of that?"

"Yes," Victor answered, proud of his arrogance. "I'm sure."

The transformation that Charles had experienced in the tomb proved to be real. He'd worried that it might turn out to be nothing more than an ephemeral rush of sentimentality or nobility. But by the third day after his trip to the mausoleum, the sense of tranquil resolve he'd felt that day had strengthened rather than dwindled.

At the core of his tranquility was a conviction of his own goodness. Pete had been right: God made him the way he was, a lover of men. And his nature was a blessing, not a curse. It took falling in love to show him this truth. Christ had never abandoned him. Christ had led him to love. Charles felt deep gratitude, and he wanted every one of his parishioners to know this kind of salvation. He served his flock with new enthusiasm. And new joy.

One month after he had emerged from the tomb a changed man, Charles awoke one morning to find a note from Kyle slipped under his living room door. It was to say goodbye. His heart felt pain, but no bitterness. Unsure whether to believe the message, he jumped on his Vespa and sped to the mansion in the Garden

District. He found the front gate wide open. He climbed the portico steps and peered through the window. The front room was empty. The walls, once covered with paintings from the plantation home, were bare.

It was true. His beloved was gone. Maybe he would never see Kyle again. His eyes filled. *God, be with him*, he whispered in his mind.

Finally collecting himself, he climbed down the porch steps without looking back and boarded his Vespa. The sun suddenly broke through the clouds, and he felt its warmth on his back and arms as he sped back to his office.

Outside the door, he found the woman from the Gentilly neighborhood waiting for him.

"I wanted to tell you, Father," she said, her green eyes bright with excitement. "Three more neighbors have moved back into their houses on my street. They want you to come and consecrate their houses, too. I'm so happy! I just believe the neighborhood's gonna rise from the dead. All of New Orleans is gonna rise from the dead. Isn't it wonderful?" Her eyes filled with tears of happiness.

Charles embraced her. When she'd gone, he rode over to Gentilly to see the new life for himself.